Praise for

News of the World

"*News of the World* is . . . [an] exquisite book about the joys of freedom . . . the discovery of unexpected, proprietary love between two people who have never experienced anything like it; pure adventure in the wilds of an untamed Texas; and the reconciling of vastly different cultures. . . . That's a lot to pack into a short . . . vigorous volume, but Ms. Jiles is capable of saying a lot in few words."
                                                              —*New York Times*

"Jiles' lyrical style and minimal punctuation allow the reader to become immersed in the dusty Texan landscape, witnessing the anguish, fear, compassion, and joy in the unlikely pair's journey."
                                                              —*Booklist* (starred review)

"A stunning story that tore at my heart and my gut. The relationship at its core between a grizzled old man and a lost young girl digs deep into what it means to care about someone and to find your place in the world."
                            —Tracy Chevalier, author of *Girl with a Pearl Earring*

"Paulette Jiles' spare Western . . . packs a powerful punch. And, boy, can Jiles write. . . . [*News of the World*] is surprisingly tender, but never soft. It's lovely." —*USA Today* (4 out of 4 stars)

"This Western is not to be missed by Jiles's fans and lovers of Texan historical fiction."
                                                              —*Library Journal*

"[A] sleek and entertaining novel. . . . What stands out amid the gun smoke and the period detail is the moving friendship between a girl with no place to fit in and an old man who has outlived his usefulness. Add them to the list of the Wild West's great odd couples." —*Wall Street Journal*

"A powerful, richly realized journey. . . . Captain Kidd belongs in the pantheon of great Western characters along with *True Grit*'s Rooster Cogburn and *Lonesome Dove*'s Gus and Call."
—Charles Frazier, National Book
Award–winning author of *Cold Mountain*

"A beautifully written story. . . . Jiles writes with great sensitivity . . . [and] conveys in sparse language the emotions of each of these perfectly drawn characters, building to a remarkable conclusion." —*BookPage*

"Jiles delivers a taut, evocative story of post–Civil War Texas in this riveting drama of a redeemed captive of the Kiowa tribe. . . . Jiles unfolds the stories of the Captain and Johanna, past and present, with the smooth assuredness of a burnished fireside tale, demonstrating that she is a master of the western."
—*Publishers Weekly*

News of the World

NEWS

OF THE

WORLD

—◆—

A NOVEL

PAULETTE

JILES

wm

WILLIAM MORROW
An Imprint of HarperCollins*Publishers*

P.S.™ is a trademark of HarperCollins Publishers.

HarperCollins books may be purchased for educational, business, or sales promotional use. For information please e-mail the Special Markets Department at SPsales@harpercollins.com.

A hardcover edition of this book was published in 2016 by William Morrow, an imprint of HarperCollins Publishers.

FIRST WILLIAM MORROW PAPERBACK EDITION PUBLISHED 2017.
FIRST WILLIAM MORROW MOVIE TIE-IN EDITION PUBLISHED 2020.

Designed by Fritz Metsch
Map by Nick Springer,
copyright © 2016 Springer Cartographics LLC

Cover Image © 2020 Universal Studios. All Rights Reserved.

Library of Congress Cataloging-in-Publication Data has been applied for.

ISBN 978-0-06-301195-3 (movie tie-in)

20 21 22 23 24   OV/LSC   10 9 8 7 6 5 4 3 2 1

For friends on the long trails:
Susan, June, April, Nancy, Caroline, Wanda,
Evelyn, and Rita Wightman Whippet

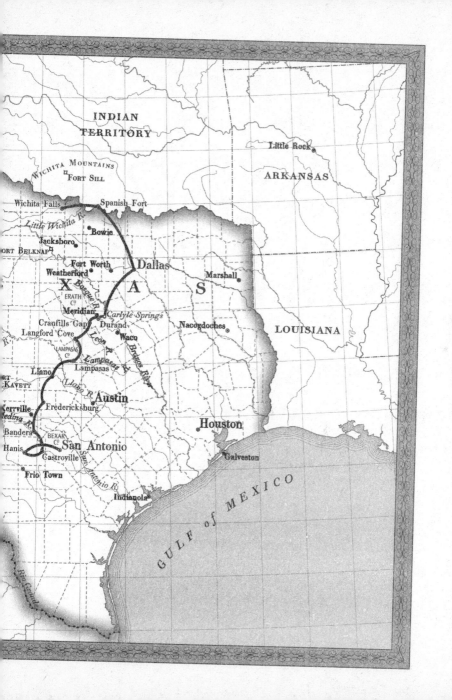

ONE

Wichita Falls, Texas, Winter 1870

CAPTAIN KIDD LAID out the *Boston Morning Journal* on the lectern and began to read from the article on the Fifteenth Amendment. He had been born in 1798 and the third war of his lifetime had ended five years ago and he hoped never to see another but now the news of the world aged him more than time itself. Still he stayed his rounds, even during the cold spring rains. He had been at one time a printer but the war had taken his press and everything else, the economy of the Confederacy had fallen apart even before the surrender and so he now made his living in this drifting from one town to another in North Texas with his newspapers and journals in a waterproof portfolio and his coat collar turned up against the weather. He rode a very good horse and was concerned that someone might try to take the horse from him but so far so good. So he had arrived in Wichita Falls on February 26 and tacked up his posters and put on his reading clothes in the stable. There was a hard rain outside and it was noisy but he had a good strong voice.

He shook out the *Journal*'s pages.

The Fifteenth Amendment, he read, which has just been rat-ified on February 3, 1870, allows the vote to all men qualified to vote without regard to race or color or previous condition of servitude. He looked up from the text. His reading glasses caught the light. He bent slightly forward over the lectern. That means colored gentlemen, he said. Let us have no vaporings or girlish shrieks. He turned his head to search the crowd of faces turned up to him. I can hear you muttering, he said. Stop it. I hate muttering.

He glared at them and then said, Next. The Captain shook out another newspaper. The latest from the *New-York Tribune* states that the polar exploration ship *Hansa* is reported by a whaler as being crushed and sunk in the pack ice in its attempt to reach the North Pole; sunk at seventy degrees north latitude off Greenland. There is nothing in this article about survivors. He flipped the page impatiently.

The Captain had a clean-shaven face with runic angles, his hair was perfectly white, and he was still six feet tall. His hair shone in the single hot ray from the bull's-eye lantern. He car-ried a short-barreled Slocum revolver in his waistband at the back. It was a five-shot, .32 caliber and he had never liked it all that much but then he had rarely used it.

Over all the bare heads he saw Britt Johnson and his men, Paint Crawford and Dennis Cureton, at the back wall. They were free black men. Britt was a freighter and the other two were his driving crew. They held their hats in their hands, each with one booted foot cocked up against the wall behind them. The hall was full. It was a broad open space used for wool storage and community meetings and for people like himself. The crowd was almost all men, almost all white. The lantern lights were harsh, the air was dark. Captain Kidd traveled from town to town in North Texas with his newspapers and read aloud the news of the day to assemblies like this in halls or churches for a dime a head. He traveled alone and had no one to collect the dimes for him but not many people cheated and if they did somebody caught them at it and grabbed them by the lapels and wrenched them up in a knot and said, *You really ought to pay your goddamn dime, you know, like everybody else.*

And then the coin would ring in the paint can.

HE GLANCED UP to see Britt Johnson lift a forefinger to him. Captain Kidd gave one brief nod, and completed his reading with an article from the *Philadelphia Inquirer* concerning the British physicist James Maxwell and his theories of electromagnetic disturbances in the ether whose wavelengths were longer than infrared radiation. This was to bore people and calm them down and put them into a state of impatience to leave—leave quietly. He had become impatient of trouble and other people's emotions. His life seemed to him thin and sour, a bit spoiled, and it was something that had only come upon him lately. A slow dullness had seeped into him like coal gas and he did not know what to do about it except seek out quiet and solitude. He was always impatient to get the readings over with now.

The Captain folded the papers, put them in his portfolio. He bent to his left and blew out the bull's-eye lantern. As he walked through the crowd people reached out to him and shook his hand. A pale-haired man sat watching him. With him were two Indians or half-Indians that the Captain knew for Caddos and not people of a commendable reputation. The man with the blond hair turned in his chair to stare at Britt. Then others came to thank the Captain for his readings, asked after his grown children. Kidd nodded, said, *Tolerable, tolerable,* and made his way back to Britt and his men to see what it was Britt wanted.

CAPTAIN KIDD THOUGHT it was going to be about the Fifteenth Amendment but it was not.

Yes sir, Captain Kidd, would you come with me? Britt straightened and lifted his hat to his head and so did Dennis and Paint. Britt said, I got a problem in my wagon.

She seemed to be about ten years old, dressed in the horse Indians' manner in a deerskin shift with four rows of elk teeth sewn across the front. A thick blanket was pulled over her shoulders. Her hair was the color of maple sugar and in it she wore two down puffs bound onto a lock of her hair by their minute spines and also bound with a thin thread was a wing-feather from a golden eagle slanting between them. She sat perfectly composed, wearing the feather and a necklace of glass beads as if they were costly adornments. Her eyes were blue and her skin that odd bright color that occurs when fair skin has been burned and weathered by the sun. She had no more expression than an egg.

I see, said Captain Kidd. I see.

He had his black coat collar turned up against the rain and the cold and a thick wool muffler around his neck. His breath moved out of his nose in clouds. He bit his lower lip on the left side and thought about what he was looking at in the light of the kerosene hurricane lantern Britt held up. In some strange way it made his skin crawl.

I am astonished, he said. The child seems artificial as well as malign.

Britt had backed one of his wagons under the roof of the fairway at the livery stable. It didn't fit all the way in. The front half of the wagon and the driver's seat was wild with the drumming noise of the rain and a bright lift of rain-spray surrounded it. The back end was under shelter and they all stood there and regarded the girl the way people do when they come upon something strange they have caught in a trap, something alien whose taxonomy is utterly unknown and probably dangerous. The girl sat on a bale of Army shirts. In the light of the lantern her eyes reflected a thin and glassy blue. She watched them, she watched every movement, every lift of a hand. Her eyes moved but her head was still.

Yes sir, said Britt. She's jumped out of the wagon twice between Fort Sill and here. As far as Agent Hammond can figure out she is Johanna Leonberger, captured at age six four years ago, from near Castroville. Down near San Antonio.

I know where it is, said Captain Kidd.

Yes sir. The Agent had all the particulars. If that's her, she's about ten.

Britt Johnson was a tall, strong man but he watched the girl with a dubious and mistrusting expression. He was cautious of her.

My name is Cicada. My father's name is Turning Water. My mother's name is Three Spotted. I want to go home.

But they could not hear her because she had not spoken

aloud. The Kiowa words in all their tonal music lived in her head like bees.

Captain Kidd said, Do they know who her parents are?

Yes sir, they do. Or as much as he can figure out from the date she was taken. The Agent, here, I'm talking about. Her parents and her little sister were killed in the raid. He had a paper from her relatives, Wilhelm and Anna Leonberger, an aunt and uncle. And he gave me a fifty-dollar gold piece to deliver her back to Castroville. The family sent it up to him by a major from San Antonio, transferred north. He was to give it to somebody to transport her home. I said I would get her out of Indian Territory and across the Red. It wasn't easy. We like to drowned. That was yesterday.

The Captain said, It's come up two foot since yesterday.

I know it. Britt stood with one foot on the drawbar. The hurricane lantern burned with its irresolute light on the tailgate and shone into the interior of the freight wagon as if revealing some alien figure in a tomb.

Captain Kidd took off his hat and shook water from it. Britt Johnson had rescued at least four captives from the red men. From the Comanche, from the Kiowa, and once from the Cheyenne up north in Kansas. Britt's own wife and two children had been taken captive six years ago, in 1864, and he had gone out and got them back. Nobody knew quite how he had done it. He seemed to have some celestial protection about him when he rode out alone on the Red Rolling Plains, a place which seemed to invite both death and dangers. Britt had taken on the task of rescuing others, a dark man, cunning and strong and fast like a nightjar in the midnight air. But Britt was not going to return this girl to her parents, not even for fifty dollars in gold.

Why won't you go? said Captain Kidd. You have come this far already. Fifty dollars in gold is a considerable amount.

I figured I could find somebody to hand her off to here, Britt said. It's a three-week journey down there. Then three weeks back. I have no haulage to carry down there.

Behind him Paint and Dennis nodded. They crossed their arms in their heavy waxed-canvas slickers. Long bright crawls of water slid across the livery stable floor and took up the light of the lantern like a luminous stain and the roof shook with the percussion of drops as big as nickels.

Dennis Crawford, thin as a spider, said, We wouldn't make a dime the whole six weeks.

Unless we could get something to haul back up here, said Paint.

Shut up, Paint, said Dennis. You know people down there?

Well, all right, said Paint. I can hear you.

Britt said, There it is. I can't leave my freighting that long. I have orders to deliver. And the other thing is, if I'm caught carrying that girl it would be bad trouble. He looked the Captain straight in the eye and said, She's a white girl. You take her.

Captain Kidd felt in his breast pocket for his tobacco. He didn't find it. Britt rolled a cigarette and handed it to him and then snapped a match in his big hand. Captain Kidd had not lost any sons in the war and that was because he had all daughters. Two of them. He knew girls. He didn't know Indians but he knew girls, and what was on that girl's face was contempt.

He said, Find a family going that way, Britt. Somebody to

drown her in sweetness and light and improving lectures on deportment.

Good idea, said Britt. I thought of it already.

And so? Captain Kidd blew out smoke. The girl's eyes did not follow it. Nothing could move her gaze from the men's faces, the men's hands. She had a drizzle of freckles across her cheekbones and her fingers were blunt as noses with short nails lined in black.

Can't locate any. Hard to find somebody to trust with this.

Captain Kidd nodded. But you've delivered girls before now, he said. The Blainey girl, you got her back.

Not that far a trip. Besides I don't know those people down there. You do.

Yes, I see.

Captain Kidd had spent years in San Antonio; he had married into an old San Antonio family and he knew the way, knew the people. In North and West Texas there were many free black men, they were freighters and scouts and now after the war, the Tenth U.S. Cavalry, all black. However, the general population had not settled the matter of free black people in their minds yet. All was in flux. Flux: a soldering aid that promotes the fusion of two surfaces, an unstable substance that catches fire.

The Captain said, You could ask the Army to deliver her. They take charge of captives.

Not anymore, said Britt.

What would you have done if you hadn't come across me?

I don't know.

I just got here from Bowie. I could have gone south to Jacksboro.

I saw your posters when we pulled in, Britt said. It was meant.

One last thing, said Captain Kidd. Maybe she should go back to the Indians. What tribe took her?

Kiowa.

Britt was smoking as well. His foot on the drawbar was jiggling. He snorted blue fumes from his nostrils and glanced at the girl. She stared back at him. They were like two mortal enemies who could not take their eyes from one another. The endless rain hissed in a ground spray out in the street and every roof in Wichita Falls was a haze of shattered water.

And so?

Britt said, The Kiowa don't want her. They finally woke up to the fact that having a white captive gets you run down by the cav. The Agent said to bring all the captives in or he was cutting off their rations and sending the Twelfth and the Ninth out after them. They brought her in and sold her for fifteen Hudson's Bay four-stripe blankets and a set of silver dinnerware. German coin silver. They'll beat it up into bracelets. It was Aperian Crow's band brought her in. Her mother cut her arms to pieces and you could hear her crying for a mile.

Her Indian mother.

Yes, said Britt.

Were you there?

Britt nodded.

I wonder if she remembers anything. From when she was six.

No, said Britt. Nothing.

The girl still did not move. It takes a lot of strength to sit that still for that long. She sat upright on the bale of Army shirts which were wrapped in burlap, marked in stencil for Fort Belknap. Around her were wooden boxes of enamel washbasins and nails and smoked deer tongues packed in fat, a sewing machine in a crate, fifty-pound sacks of sugar. Her round face was flat in the light of the lamp and without shadows, or softness. She seemed carved.

Doesn't speak any English?

Not a word, said Britt.

So how do you know she doesn't remember anything?

My boy speaks Kiowa. He was captive with them a year.

Yes, that's right. Captain Kidd shifted his shoulders under the heavy dreadnought overcoat. It was black, like his frock coat and vest and his trousers and his hat and his blunt boots. His shirt had last been boiled and bleached and ironed in Bowie; a fine white cotton with the figure of a lyre in white silk. It was holding out so far. It was one of the little things that had been depressing him. The way it frayed gently on every edge.

He said, Your boy spoke with her.

Yes, said Britt. For as much as she'd talk to him.

Is he with you?

Yes. Better on the road with me than at home. He's good on the road. They are different when they come back. My boy nearly didn't want to come back to me.

Is that so? The Captain was surprised.

Yes sir. He was on the way to becoming a warrior. Learned the language. It's a hard language.

He was with them how long?

Less than a year.

Britt! How can that be?

I don't know. Britt smoked and turned to lean on the wagon tailgate and looked back into the dark spaces of the stable with the noise of horses and mules eating, eating, their teeth like grindstones moving one on another and the occasional snort as hay dust got up their noses, the shifting of their great cannonball feet. The good smell of oiled leather harness and grain. Britt said, I just don't know. But he came back different.

In what way?

Roofs bother him. Inside places bother him. He can't settle down and learn his letters. He's afraid a lot and then he turns around arrogant. Britt threw down his smoke and stepped on it. So, gist of it is, the Kiowa won't take her back.

Captain Kidd knew, besides the other reasons, that Britt trusted him to return her to her people because he was an old man.

Well, he said.

I knew you would, said Britt.

Yes, said the Captain. So.

Britt's skin was saddle colored but now paler than it usually was because the rainy winter had kept the sun from his face for months. He reached into the pocket of his worn ducking coat and brought out the coin. It was a shining sulky color, a Spanish coin of eight escudos in twenty-two karat gold, and all the edge still milled, not shaved. A good deal of money; everyone in Texas was counting their nickels and dimes and glad to have them since the finances of the state had collapsed and both news and hard money were difficult to come by. Especially here in North Texas, near the banks of the Red River, on the edge of Indian Territory.

Britt said, That's what the family sent up to the Agent. Her parents' names were Jan and Greta. They were killed when the Kiowa captured her. Take it, he said. And be careful of her.

As they watched, the girl slid down between the freight boxes and bales as if fainting and pulled the thick blanket over her head. She was weary of being stared at.

Britt said, She'll stay there the night. She's got nowhere to go. She can't get hold of any weapons that I can think of. He took up the lamp and stepped back. Be really careful.

TWO

———•••———

THE WOMEN OF the town of Wichita Falls gave her a blue-and-yellow-striped dress and underthings, worsted stockings, a nightgown with a lace banding at the neck, and shoes that more or less fit, but they could do nothing with her. They were reluctant to use force on a small, thin girl with scars on her forearms and a stare like a china doll. They didn't want to wrestle with the child, and in addition she had lice.

Finally the Captain took her to Lottie's establishment. The women there were bold and somehow virile, and had tramped the roads as camp followers. Many had been in jail here and there. They were not in the least reluctant to use force. It cost them two hours to get her into a bathtub and washed and to dispose of her Kiowa dress. One of the women threw the glass beads and the deerskin dress with its valuable elk teeth out the window. They pulled the feathers from her hair, which was crawling with graybacks.

They held her head under a stream of hot water from a pitcher and scrubbed her scalp and her body with blue soap. She fought with them; for ten years old she was agile, thin, amazingly strong, and soapy. Water and suds ran down the walls. At the end, the tub lay on its side and the water drained between the cracks of the floorboards into the receiving parlor below and stained the red flocking on the wallpaper while the girl's flat and glassy eyes regarded them all from the floor where she crouched. Her hair was plastered all over her head like wet strings. They wrestled her into the underthings and the dress and the stockings and the shoes.

They shoved her out the door and good riddance. The stockings were wet and twisted. The rain filled the street, making long thin lakes like stripes in the wheel tracks. The Captain held her stiff, wooden hand as they walked back to the livery stable. She did not pick up her skirt apparently because she did not know how, or did not know it was necessary. Or did not care. By the time they got to the stable the dress hems were carrying several pounds of red sludge, and she bent her head low and when she made a strangled noise he realized she was trying not to cry.

Captain Kidd bought a spring wagon from the livery stable. He bought it with the Spanish coin and was lucky to get it. It was in fact an excursion wagon painted a dark and glossy green and in gold letters on the sides it said *Curative Waters East Mineral Springs Texas* and he had no idea how the wagon had come all the way from near Houston to this little town on the Red River. The wagon surely had a story all to itself that would now remain forever unknown, untold. It was a jaunty little vehicle with two rows of seats running the length of the wagon bed so the people going to the curative mineral waters could sit and stare across at one another. There were poles to support a canopy and side curtains. This was but poor protection against hard weather but it was all he had.

He would sell the wagon in Castroville or San Antonio if he ever got there and in the meantime it would be a luxury to travel in a vehicle with a spring seat to take the ruts and the hammering. His roan mare packhorse could pull it and his bay saddle horse could come behind.

It would also allow him to keep the girl within sight. He wished he knew her name in Kiowa. He would call her Johanna, as if it mattered. She didn't know the word "Johanna" from Deuteronomy.

Captain Kidd changed to his duck coat and trousers of jeans cloth, a double-breasted plains shirt. He put on his old traveling hat with the uneven brim. He laid his black reading suit in careful layers into his carpet bag and his good black hat for readings into a tin hatbox. A hat can, as the cowboys said. Young people could get away with rough clothing but unless the elderly dressed with care they looked like homeless vagabonds and at every reading he must present the appearance of authority and wisdom.

He packed up his newspapers and his cutthroat razor and its cake of soap, the brush, his shot box with powder and caps and wads and the spring-loaded powder charger. Into the bed of the *Curative Waters* wagon he threw his shotgun, purchases of tinned butter and dried beef, bacon, two sheepskins, a small box of medical supplies, a keg of flour, water bottles, a candle lantern and candles, a small stove. Then his portfolio with his newspapers and a map of the roads of Texas, which he rarely used. Finally his riding boots and his saddle and blankets. He lifted the girl into the wagon bed and made "stay" motions with his hands. Then he went looking for Britt.

THEY WERE PARKED in front of a general merchandise store. Dennis and Paint were trying to even out their loads in both wagons. Britt's boy was there with them; he worked hard and quickly and seemed to look constantly and anxiously at his father. Dennis supervised the loading. They had to cross the upper Little Wichita and they did not want the wagons to go down by the head. Their teams were big strong bays. Admirable horses.

The Captain said, Britt, which roads are open?

Britt climbed up to the driver's seat on one wagon with his boy at his side and Dennis was at the reins in the other. Paint sat beside Dennis smoking a cigar with great enjoyment. A light rain was still drifting down into the colorless late-spring world of North Texas and its low and restless sky.

Britt said, Take the road alongside the Red east to Spanish Fort, Captain. They say it's not flooded yet, and then from Spanish Fort the southeast road to Weatherford and Dallas is good. Get to Spanish as quick as you can and away from the Red because it's still coming up. From Weatherford and Dallas you can get directions for the Meridian Road heading south.

Very well, said the Captain. I am obliged. He thought about his solitude. About his thin, lean life and the coal gas. He said, The Meridian Road heading south.

Britt had a military bearing and the attentive gaze of a man who had spent long hard months with a scouting company. He bent down from the wagon seat and held out his hand.

And sir, let me see that Slocum you got.

Captain Kidd pulled aside his threadbare canvas chore coat and reached behind and drew out the revolver. He handed it to Britt butt-first. Water dripped from his bare hand.

Britt turned it over. He said, Captain, this is the kind of thing I got for Christmas when I was ten. It doesn't even have standard charges. Britt laid the Slocum at his side and then drew out his own Smith and Wesson and handed it to the older man. I owe you, he said, for taking that maniac. What else are you carrying?

A twelve-gauge. Captain Kidd tried to keep from smiling. A younger man with all the latest devices, taking care of the doddering old.

Watch your right side.

I'm left-handed.

All the better.

Captain Kidd reached up and shook hands with Britt and watched them leave. The two long, narrow wagons were weighted with their loads and the teams of big bay horses leaned into their collars and plumed out smoke and pulled until the back bands stood up off their spines. The wheels moved through the red mud of the street at first slowly, one spoke rolling up after another. Dennis sang out to his team in his high, thin voice, *Walk on, walk on!* And Britt stood braced behind the driver's seat with the reins in his hands and his big hat flinging water and called his horses by their names encouragingly and then the two freight wagons began to move at a walking pace.

The Captain unwound his long reins from the driver's post and at first his little packhorse mare sulked and refused and danced around in the harness, which she did not like, but at last leaned forward and pulled.

The Captain called out, Am I not good to you, then, Fancy? Do I not feed you and put shoes on your feet? Move on, girl!

Several people standing out of sight in doorways watched them leave. Some were shaking their heads at the sight of the old man and the ten-year-old girl wild with dread, her new dress splattered with Red River mud and her hems coated in a slurry of iron-red mire. And there were other, more covert faces, looks of interest and of greed; the pale-haired man with his neck bound in a blue-patterned neckerchief and tobacco smoke drifting from his nose.

Britt and his two wagons went south down Childress Street toward the lower Little Wichita, and the Captain and the captive girl set out east toward Spanish Fort. The wheels threw up spinning arcs of slurry and water that planted polka dots all over the wagon sides. The Captain and Johanna would travel through the Cross Timbers to Spanish Fort and then on south to Dallas and eventually four hundred miles farther south, down into the *brasada*, the short-brush country of San Antonio, with its slow, uncoiling alluvial rivers and its great live oaks in the valleys, its slow uncoiling people.

The man with the pale hair dropped his cigar butt in a puddle. With him were the two others, Caddos who had slid in a sideways direction from the tribal lands, and as they drifted they had gathered trouble and a great deal of peculiar knowledge about human beings, what human beings would do or say under extreme duress. It was not something you could do anything with but it interested them all the same.

THREE

———◆———

THE CAPTAIN STARTED out his headlong rush toward military rank with the Georgia militia in the War of 1812, which had stretched out to 1815. He had just turned sixteen. His militia had traveled west to the Battle of Horseshoe Bend in Alabama under Jackson. Jefferson Kyle Kidd was at that point nothing but a private who had lifted his hand to vote for a man named Thompson for captain. They were sitting on piles of rails in the Georgia hill country, the day before they were to leave out. After putting their supplies, arms, ammunition, and personal kits together, then finding horses, they realized that it was necessary to hold elections for officers. That in fact they needed officers. That one had to say Yes Sir and No Sir and make a salute and present a military bearing. Two of the officers they had elected last year weren't standing and three had moved to Tennessee. They were confused as to the purpose of sergeants and corporals and so decided to forego them. He himself was a Georgia hill country person and spoke that way and thought that way for all of his life, the habits and intonation would stay with him always. He lifted his hand for Thompson.

On March 27, 1814, at the battle itself, he was hit on the outside of the right hip, leaving a long sear of fragmented flesh and torn homespun and bright red blood. He and the Georgia boys were with Coffee's forces south of the bend. They had pulled down the timbers of a cabin for breastworks. He didn't even know at first he had been shot. He was lying beside two boys from his county firing over the timbers where a large soap kettle had rolled out of the fireplace. Round after round from the Creek and Choctaw across the river struck the kettle and made it ring like a bell so that it was hard to hear Thompson lying out in front and crawling toward them, toward cover.

Finally Sherman Foster called to him, Jeff, Jeff, that's Captain Thompson out there!

The Red Sticks, the Muskogee Creek Indians, across the Tallapoosa were laying in a very accurate fire. They had the range on the cabin and the soap kettle and, he now realized, Thompson. All the Red Sticks had were smoothbores but those great .72 caliber balls could kill you just as dead as a rifled gun. The barrels of their guns on the other side of the river looked as long as wagon tongues. He wrapped the firing mechanism of his flintlock rifle in his kerchief and laid it down in the sand. He pulled the powder horn and powder-measure strap off over his head. Shucked off his cartridge box and crawled out to get his captain. Even though it was late March the Alabama sun blazed and roasted everything in its light. The river itself was like some kind of running metal. The smoke of their firing lay in planes. There was no wind. Now Thompson was silent. Why had he gone out there, past the barricade? Everything was the color of a biscuit, the color of yellow sunlight and the sulphur shades of gunpowder smoke.

He slid between two collapsed timbers and when he reached for Thompson's outflung arm the sand erupted around him as if tiny explosive charges had been set underground. The firing was continuous. He laid hold of the bloodied arm and its torn shirt-sleeve and dragged Thompson back into the shelter of the criss-crossed cabin timbers. He pulled him over a broken mirror and a calendar and some spoons. Thompson's boot heels caught the calendar and its pages rolled over—March and April and May.

When he got him back under cover the captain was dying. It was a strange thing to roll a man's body over on its back and look for signs of life. A thing invisible. He had been hit in the V of his throat. *Where've you been all the day, Randall my son? O Mother, make my bed soon for I am sick to my heart, and I fain would lie doon.* He had heard that song all his life and now he knew what it meant. He tore open Thompson's military jacket, his shirt; he saw life draining away, draining away.

You're hit, Sherman said. Look at you, you're hit.

I am? Jefferson Kyle Kidd, sixteen years old last week, lay back in the yellow dirt and looked down his own body, the homespun brown pants and square-toed boots and his lanky long legs, the spreading red stain on the outside of his right hip. The weave of the homespun had been driven into his flesh. I'm all right, he said. It's all right.

Later they had to pull his pants off and truss up the bandage around his hip bone and his crotch, which was embarrassing, but it healed well.

He was elected sergeant because they were told they needed
one. Sherman moved up to lieutenant and Hezekiah Pitt was
made captain to replace Thompson. So there he was with a
rank he knew nothing about.

After the battle he sat in a tent with some of the officers of
the Thirty-ninth U.S. Infantry to ask them about the duties of
a sergeant and made a list. He was anxious to do well and to get
everything right. They laughed at him; elected sergeant and not
even twenty years old yet. Such was the militia. They laughed
at the way he spoke. They were men from Maine and New York,
they said *noiss* and *reaftah* and *keaf.* He bent tight to the paper
so they could not see his puzzled expression and eventually figured out these words meant *nurse* and *rafter* and *calf.*

He wrote down, in a neat list, all the obligations of a sergeant
because written information was what mattered in this world,
from after-action reports to scout maps to the list of company
clerk duties. Then the Georgia and Tennessee militias and
the Army regulars started out for Pensacola. They were in the
country the people called Alabama, and the United States government called Mississippi Territory.

Since he had carried himself well at the Battle of Horseshoe
Bend and was of age he was forwarded to the Thirty-ninth Provost Marshall's Department. They needed him. He was a big
tall cracker. It was a long march to Pensacola. They marched
south out of the Alabama hill country and down into the saw-
grass country, through wastes of fan palm standing at a height
to rake at his hip wound, all of it covered in green briar vines
that grew thorns on every inch of their whipcord trailers and all
along the march the company musician played "Stone Grinds

All" and "Little Drops of Brandy" on his breathless Irish tin whistle in the key of D, over and over. At Pensacola the Army put him to transporting prisoners. He hated it.

He learned all the devices of interrogation and the secret codes with which his British prisoners communicated with one another, how to use wrestling holds on a fighting prisoner, a thumb lock. He learned the uses of manacles and leg irons, the maintenance of prisons in the hot sands of the Florida gulf. Within a few months he talked his way out of the Provost Marshall's unit and its commanding officer's managerial hands and into the message corps. The runners.

Then at last he was doing what he loved: carrying information by hand alone through the Southern wilderness; messages, orders, maps, reports. Jackson's army had no other signal capacity, not like the Navy. Captain Kidd was already over six feet tall and he had a runner's muscles. He had good lungs and he knew the country. He was from Ball Ground, Georgia, in the Blue Ridge, and covering ground at a long trot was meat and drink to him.

At that time his hair was a deep brown tied up in a pigtail and nothing pleased him more than to travel free and unencumbered, alone, with a message in his hand, carrying information from one unit to another, unconcerned with its content, independent of what was written or ordered therein. He ran at the far fringe of Jackson's Tennessee Regulars and their crossed white bandoliers. He saluted the adjutant at a staff tent, received instructions, stuffed the messages in his bag, and he was off.

A lifting, running joy. He felt like a thin banner streaming, printed with some regal insignia with messages of great import entrusted to his care. He was given a runner's corps badge made of silvery metal. He smeared bacon fat on it and dusted it over so it would not shine and give him away as he jogged on through the hills, through the sand and fan palms of the coast. They gave him a flintlock pistol to carry but it was heavy and the gooseneck cock was always catching on something so he pulled the load and carried it in his knapsack.

He dodged artillery and musket fire at Fort Bowyer in Mobile and then back across the Georgia line to Cumberland Island with his messages in a leather budget both on foot and riding those little Florida horses called Tackies. Two years of directed flight across Georgia and the Alabama country, solitary, with his information in hand. Once he fell asleep exhausted in a big empty ash hopper by a cabin to wake up and find himself in a farmyard full of Brits. He stayed where he was until it was hot noontime, when they all left. If they had discovered him they would have shot him dead in the hopper.

He always recalled those two years with a kind of wonder. As when one is granted the life and the task for which one was meant. No matter how odd, no matter how out of the ordinary. When it came to an end he was not surprised. It was too good, too perfect to last.

He wanted then to go west to the Spanish settlements but he had a widowed mother and younger sisters to look after and to provide for. He was not a man to marry without due deliberation. Twice he deliberated too long and the young women returned his letters and married others. By the time he completed his apprenticeship to a printer in Macon his mother had died and both sisters finally married. After Santa Ana had shot up San Antonio and burned the bodies of Travis and his men at the Alamo and then got whipped at San Jacinto, he left for Texas.

The second war was President Tyler's war with Mexico. By that time Jefferson Kidd was nearly fifty and had long settled into life in San Antonio, where he finally met his wife. He had set up his press in the Plaza de Las Islas, which was also called Main Plaza, on the first floor of a new modern building belonging to a lawyer named Branholme. He found type with tildas and the aigu accent and the upside down exclamation and question marks. He studied Spanish so he could print whatever circulars and broadsheets were needed, many for the Cathedral parish. The San Antonio newspaper fed him a great deal of business, as did the hay market and the saloons.

Often on his long rides about Texas with his newspapers in his portfolio and the portfolio in his saddlebags, the Captain fell into memories of his wife. The first day he ever saw Maria Luisa Betancort y Real. This was how the Captain knew that things of the imagination were often as real as those you laid your hand upon. And as for making her acquaintance, seeing and meeting were two different things. She was of an old Spanish family and formal arrangements had to be made for an introduction. There is a repeat mechanism in the human mind that operates independently of will. The memory brought with it the vacuity of loss, irremediable loss, and so he told himself he would not indulge himself in memory but it could not be helped. She was running down Soledad after the milkman and his buckskin horse. The milkman's name was Policarpo and he had passed by her family's house without stopping. *Poli! Poli!*

She lost a shoe running. She had gray eyes. They were the color of rain. Her hair was curly. Her family's house was the big *casa de dueña* of the Betancort family at the intersection of Soledad and Dolorosa. The corner of Sad and Lonely.

The Captain walked out of his print shop and took the buckskin's halter. Poli, stop, he said. A *señorita* wants you. So he recalled it anyway, against his will, every bead on her sash fringe and her hand on his arm to balance herself as she wormed her thin, small foot back into the shoe and then the warm milk pouring into her jug. The milk smelled like cow, the vanilla scent of the whitebrush that the milk cows loved to eat on the banks of Calamares Creek. Her gray eyes.

So he became a man with a wife and two daughters. He loved print, felt something right about sending out information into the world. Independent of its content. He had a Stanhope press and a shop with nine-foot windows that allowed all the light he needed onto the casings and the plates and layout tables. During the Mexican War they said they needed him anyway, even at his age. He was to organize the communications of Taylor's forces and was given a small hand press to print orders of the day. He had never seen a hand press so small. He wrote up Taylor's orders and handed them to Captain Walker of the Texas Rangers and Walker's horsemen galloped with messages between Port Isabel on the Gulf to the Army encampment north of Matamoros, on the Rio Grande.

At one point an aide-de-camp on Taylor's staff came up with the idea of sending up a hot-air balloon to spy on Arista's lines and drop propaganda. Finally someone else pointed out that one good shot would bring the balloon down. Others pointed out that most of the Mexican recruits could not read. A lieutenant-colonel quashed the brainstorm. Never underestimate the ingenuity of the U.S. Army.

Taylor made him a brevet captain in the Second Division so he could organize the couriers and get what he needed: paper, ink, horses. His service in the War of 1812 recommended him for the rank. Ever afterward he was known as Captain Kidd.

And so he was at Resaca de la Palma when one of Arista's twelve-pound balls came through the staff tent and shattered a table into fragments three feet from him. Oil from the lamps jumped into great transparent dots on the canvas. A major stood arrested with a table splinter through his neck. This collar is too tight, he said, and fainted. Against all odds he lived.

He heard the *centinela alerto* as the men crashed through Arista's lines and saw them come back cheering with their loot; the Mexican general's table silver and his writing desk and the colors of the Tampico Battalion. What is the use of winning a battle without loot? You overwhelm them and take their stuff—military basics.

He was with Taylor's forces at Buena Vista, in the high mountains above Monterrey. They had been shot at all the way from the Rio Grande by either Mexican Army sharpshooters or Apaches, it was a toss-up as to which. The Captain was handed a Model 1830 Springfield flintlock but he had been raised with them and knew them well. He lay in a wagon bed and fired at the gunsmoke and, he hoped, brought down more than one hidden sniper. It was the middle of February of 1847. In the thin air of the mountains outside that Mexican town, with smoke from their campfires rising straight up in the still air, the young men wanted to know about the Battle of Horseshoe Bend. They wanted to compare their own behavior with that of their forebears. They wanted to know if they measured up, if what they endured was as difficult, if their enemies were as cunning and as brave.

The Texas Rangers lounged against the caissons and listened. They were cool young men and utterly reckless and apparently without fear. The Mexicans hated them and called them *rinches* but if they could have fielded an independent cavalry wing as skilled and as lethal they would have, but they didn't, and so there you were.

The Captain had never met any troops or unit like them. They listened out of courtesy to an older man. And so in the cold night under the high stars of Mexico, he told them what he could. Or what he felt like telling. The Creek and the Choctaw were using smoothbores, he said. His Georgia militia company brought their own rifles and used minie balls, that on their way to Pensacola their wagons had sunk hub-deep in the sand. That his captain had got killed on the second day of the battle and he managed to crawl out and drag him back under cover but he died. And quickly went on: that Jackson was a fearless man, he was a maniac when he was fighting. The question hung unasked in the air: Were you wounded?

And yes, I got shot in the hip, he said. Didn't hit the bone. I didn't know it until later. The Red Sticks had run out of ammunition and they were firing all kinds of things out of those smoothbores. I think I got hit with a spoon.

He paused. The knees of his trousers smoked from the heat

of the fire and his hands were stained with ink. At that time he carried a new Colt revolver and it dragged and was heavy at his belt. The Rangers smoked and waited in silence in the shadow of their hats. Their beards were silky because they were young but when you looked at their faces it seemed they were artificially aged in some way.

They wanted some wisdom, some advice.

You can get hit and not know it, he said. So could the man next to you. Take care of one another.

They nodded and stared at the fire and thought about it. They thought about fighting now in a strange land and against a strange army, one that was stiffly European and formal where the barefoot mestizo privates still were forced to wear neck stocks. Their own opponent was José Mariano Martín Buenaventura Ignacio Nepomuceno García de Arista Nuez, who was a fiercely committed republican and at odds with his own general staff. The Mexican Army was in fact torn into factions by immovable aristocrats and generals with liberal theories.

Afterward, late, when he was alone and the fire of mesquite wood was dying, it came to him that he should take on the task of dispensing these interesting, nay, *vital* facts gleaned from the intelligence reports and the general press. For instance, the struggles going on at the top levels of the Mexican Army. If people had true knowledge of the world perhaps they would not take up arms and so perhaps he could be an aggregator of information from distant places and then the world would be a more peaceful place. He had been perfectly serious. That illusion had lasted from age forty-nine to age sixty-five.

And then he had come to think that what people needed, at bottom, was not only information but tales of the remote, the mysterious, dressed up as hard information. And he, like a runner, immobile in his smeared printing apron bringing it to them. Then the listeners would for a small space of time drift away into a healing place like curative waters.

FOUR

———◆◆———

S HE WALKED ALONGSIDE the wagon, singing. *Ausay gya kii,
gyao boi tol.* Prepare for a hard winter, prepare for hard times.
She walked beside the horse barefoot with the soles of her small
feet hard as wood. Like all people who do not wear shoes her big
toes pointed straight ahead. *Ausay gya kii,* she sang.

As far as she knew she was walking into disaster, into a land
blighted and starved. All around in the rolling hills there were
neither buffalo nor canyon wrens with their spilling of song. In
this land there were no Kiowa or mother or father. She was utterly alone, trapped in peculiar clothing, a dress made of cloth
with blue and yellow stripes and a tight waist. She had been
laced into a thing that she could only imagine was for magical
purposes, meant to confine her heart and her breath in a sort of
cage to hold her forever like a shut fist that would never open.

She put her hand on the shaft of the wagon and sang as
she walked because it was better than weeping. The land was
covered with the short, contorted oaks of the Red River valley, their limbs all so black with rain. The earth rolled loose
on either side as if it had been released from the confinement

of towns. It was a puzzling thing as to why they packed up in towns in the way they did. She carried her shoes around her neck with the laces tied together and walked in the felting of wet leaves. She would find out where they were going and then either escape or starve herself to death. It was not worth being alive when one was alone among aliens. People who would kill you, who had killed your dear ones. The Agent had said she was going back to her people. As far as she could tell he was not making a joke.

The Captain sat in the driver's seat of the wagon with his coat collar turned up and the brim of his old field hat down over his forehead. A light drizzle drifted through the landscape of cranky post oak trees whose limbs did not have six inches of straight in any of them. The road rose and fell on the short and choppy hills on the south bank of the Red. His bay saddle horse, Pasha, was tied at the rear of the wagon to a ringbolt and sauntered along, happy and free of a rider. His packhorse, Fancy, was now between the shafts; she had been broken to harness and went along well enough. She looked longingly from one side of the two-track road to the other at the tufts of grass, now just coming up green in late February. To their left was the Red River, a wide sheet of water the color of brick. He pulled up.

He motioned to the girl. She stood beside the packhorse and gripped the harness. She stared at him and did not come any closer.

Look here, he said. He pulled out the Smith and Wesson. He clicked the cartridge cylinder loose and flipped it out, showed her the charges. With a twist of his hand he snapped it back into place. He said, This is in case there's trouble. He stared about himself in a theatrical manner, mimed caution, held out the revolver toward the trees and made shooting noises. He put it back on the wagon floorboards on his left side with a broad, obvious gesture.

She was still, unmoving. Only her eyes moved.

And this, he said. He pulled out the old shotgun. He reached into the wagon box and took out a handful of shells. He said, In case of attack, this completely inadequate load of bird shot will make a loud noise, if nothing else. The girl watched carefully, confused, as he lifted the shotgun and then her face cleared. He had been holding the shotgun and the revolver left-handed. The Captain turned the shotgun muzzle in every direction with his deep hawk's eyes squinted down the barrel.

He put everything back. He didn't smile at her. He knew better. She stood still as a fallen leaf. He sat, lanky and tall, on the driver's seat and regarded the girl with a calm look until finally she gave him one sharp nod. It seemed to him she understood but was not willing to concede they might be on the same side against anyone or anything.

They went on. He thought about her oddness. What was it that made the girl so strange? She had none of the gestures or expressions of white people. White people's faces were mobile and open. They were unguarded. They flung their hands about, they slanted and leaned on things, tossed their heads and their hats. Her faultless silence made her seem strangely not present. She had the carriage of every Indian he had ever seen and there was a sort of kinetic stillness about them and yet she was a ten-year-old girl with dark blond hair in streaks and blue eyes and freckles.

You, he said, and pointed at her.

She made a small, slight dodging motion to one side. Her loose biscuit-colored hair flew in a wave. Kiowa people never pointed with their fingers. Never. They pointed with gun barrels and with the shaman sticks that threw venomous demons into an enemy's body. Otherwise not. He could not know that.

You, Jo-han-ah, he said. You, Johanna.

She was leaning slightly forward from the waist as if this would help her understand. She held on to the roan mare's back band. The rich scent of the horse and its warm anatomy was the only thing familiar to her in this catastrophic change in her life.

Captain. He pointed to himself.

She walked sideways in order to look at him and after a minute or so she understood that this pointing might not do any harm. He could not be throwing the demons into himself. Surely not.

He tried again. He sat quietly with the reins in his right hand and with his left he pointed to her again. Johanna, he said, patiently. He made an encouraging gesture. He waited.

She let go of the back band and stood still and held up both hands in front of herself with the palms out. He pulled up the little roan mare. She called on her guardian spirit, the one who had told her she must wear two down puffs in her hair along with a golden eagle wing feather as a sign that he would always be with her. They had taken them away. They had thrown it all out a window. But her guardian spirit might still hear her. The old man wanted her to say some enchanted naming word. It might not be harmful.

She said, Chohenna. When she spoke her lower teeth showed white.

He pointed to himself. Captain, he said.

Kep-dun, she said.

He pointed to her again.

She stiffened a moment in fear but gathered her courage and said, Chohenna.

Then he pointed to himself again.

She said, Kep-dun.

Very well. Now, we'll go on.

THEY CROSSED THE upper Little Wichita only a mile from where it ran into the Red River and they crossed it at a run. The Captain lifted Johanna into the wagon bed, pulled Pasha's lead rope loose and let him go. He found the camp knife, a butcher knife, and stuck it sheath and all into his belt in case he might have to cut Fancy out of her harness. They started a quarter-mile from the crossing at a fast trot and then hit the water at a gallop. Johanna clung to the long seats and waves of spray battered the *Curative Waters East Mineral Springs Texas* gold letters. They slowed as the current stopped them and then it took hold of the little mare and their wagon as well. Crows shot up out of the far bank screaming. Foam churned around them, drift and duff ran on top of the fast water in snaking lines. Briefly the wagon floated. The roan mare snorted, went under, came up and beat at the floodwaters with her hooves. Then she struck hard bottom and they pulled up on the far bank with water draining in streams. Pasha was a constitutionally brave horse and he plunged in after them without hesitation and struck out and came out a few yards downstream with triumphant little tosses of his head. He shook himself in a flying halo of spray and came trotting to join them and was retied to the wagon. As they went on the Captain cocked his head and listened to a steady clicking sound. He got down and looked at the front wheel. There was a break in the iron tire. Nothing to do about it now; maybe there would be a blacksmith in Spanish Fort.

THAT NIGHT THE Captain demonstrated to her the little sheet-iron stove he had bought along with the wagon. It would make less smoke than a campfire. It was the size of a large ammunition box with a small chimney going up two feet or so, enough to keep smoke out of their faces. He let down the tailgate and patted the stove where it sat, square and black and forbidding.

She had no idea what it was for.

Stove, he said. Fire. He fitted the pipes.

She stood in front of it in her yellow-and-blue-striped dress, her bare feet, the bright taffy-colored hair streaming down her back, damp with the drizzle. In a swift motion she suddenly carried her right arm down in front of herself and then snapped her fingers upward in a blossom of hard nails and calluses.

Ah, said the Captain. Sign. The sign for fire. He knew a bit of the Plains Indians sign language and so he made the sign for Yes.

This was encouraging. They at least had some limited means of speech.

He showed her how the stove worked—the top lid the size of a hand, the draft wheel. He strung up one of the wagon's side curtains between a short, warped post oak and the wagon side to make a shelter against the drizzle. She watched his every move. Perhaps she was afraid, perhaps she knew she had to learn how these things worked.

The horses were happy with their morales, feed bags holding a hefty portion of shelled corn. The girl stood beside the little mare and ran her hand down the horse's leg. She made a little pitying noise. The mare was young and strong but she had a slightly twisted right foreleg, the hoof turned inward several degrees and because of this the Captain had got her cheap. The girl had spotted it immediately and she patted the mare gently as she and Pasha stood side by side and ground up their corn with a noise like hand grinders.

The Captain found dry sticks in the clusters of tall bear grass and fished his match safe out of his inner coat pocket. He did everything slowly and deliberately. He started the fire. Johanna watched with a cautious expression, a mistrustful look. She bent toward the little stove to peer in the grate and saw the air sucked into it to make the sticks burn with more intensity. Cautiously she patted the top and then snatched her hand back.

Pi tso ha!

Yes, he said. Whatever that means. Hot, I suppose.

He made up coffee and a corn dodger and fried bacon. She sat under the canvas side curtain with her food in her hands for a long time. At last she sang over it, as if adoring it, as if the bacon were a live being and the smoking dodger a gift from the Corn Woman. There was no campfire to throw shadows but there was a half-moon waxing and it seemed to run in reverse between cascading clouds that flowed together and then pulled apart and then ran together again.

The Captain wiped his plate with the cornbread. She might run. She had nowhere to go, however. The Kiowa were across the river and the river was a loose and moving ocean of foaming rusty floodwater nearly half a mile wide that carried off entire trees. She might lay hands on the revolver or the shotgun, and he could wake up in the next world.

The Captain lay back on his old Spanish saddle that he had turned upside down, his head pillowed on the fleecing. He brought out the *Chicago Tribune* and flipped through it by the light of the candle in the candle lantern. She lay rolled in a thick serape called a *jorongo* in a red-and-black diamond pattern and stared at him with her open, flat blue eyes.

He rattled the pages and said, There's a big new packing plant in Chicago. Astounding, isn't it? They feed the cattle in at one end and at the other end they come out in cans.

She never took her eyes from him. He knew she was prepared for some kind of violence. Captain Kidd was a man old not only in years but in wars. He smiled at her at last and took out his pipe. More than ever knowing in his fragile bones that it was the duty of men who aspired to the condition of humanity to protect children and kill for them if necessary. It comes to a person most clearly when he has daughters. He had thought he was done raising daughters. As for protecting this feral child he was all for it in principle but wished he could find somebody else to do it.

You are an immense amount of trouble, he said. We will both be happy when you are with your relatives and you can make their lives a living hell.

Her face did not change. She wiped her nose slowly on her sleeve.

He turned the page. He said, This is writing. This is print-ing. This tells us of all the things we ought to know in the world. And also that we ought to want to know. He glanced over at her. He said, There are places in the world called England and Eu-rope and In-di-a. He blew smoke from his nose. He probably should not be smoking. You could smell it for miles.

In-di-a, she whispered. She began to place her fingertips to-gether one by one.

He lay back in his blankets and said his prayers for Britt, who was always in harm's way in his travels. For the safety of his daughters and son-in-law and the grandsons, perhaps soon to travel, at his request, the long and perilous journey from Geor-gia. This would include crossing the Mississippi. For his own safety and that of Johanna, also in harm's way.

So many people, so much harm.

He put his hat over his face and after a while he fell asleep.

FIVE

———◆———

THE NEXT DAY they went on toward Spanish Fort. The road wound along the south edge of the river in the great valley of the Red. More than a mile away south was the rise of land and the bluffs. At some distant time the river had been there, tearing away land; over the centuries it moved like a big red snake from one side of its valley to the other. The rain had stopped for now.

The Captain was unhappy about her walking but she would not ride nor would she put on her shoes. She watched the river. She well knew that on the other side was Indian Territory. Her mother was over there, her father, perhaps brothers and sisters and all her kin group, her clan within the tribe, perhaps a young man to whom she might have been promised. The black trunks of the live oak were twisted and wiry as chimney brushes. A good place for an ambush. He wished he had a dog. He should have got a dog from somebody.

She stopped and held up her hand. She was looking ahead.

He twitched the long reins and Fancy stopped. Behind them Pasha pointed his ears ahead and suddenly called out in a long, ringing cry.

Captain Kidd pulled out the revolver and once again checked his loads. All dry. He laid it beside him on the floorboards next to the wagon seat on the left side and covered it with a canvas-wrapped flitch of bacon. He reminded himself that the .38 cartridges were hidden in the flour keg.

After a few moments he heard the sound of about ten horses, and the jingling of bits and saddle gear. Their shod hooves clicked on the stones of the road. A company of U.S. Army mounted infantry rode into view a quarter of a mile down the road.

He jumped down and grabbed the girl by the upper arm. He made the sign for "good" in front of her face. They were on one of the few straight and level stretches between all the thick post oak and the soldiers came toward him and Johanna in a unit of blue and of flashing well-shined leather, appearing out of the trees like ghost soldiers. He turned her to him and made the sign for "friend." She had turned the color of pastry. Her lips were trembling. He led her to the wagon wheel and lifted her so that she put one bare foot on a spoke and then sprang up into the wagon bed and sank down in a welter of skirts and loose hair. She pulled the thick wool *jorongo* over her head. He came up after her, sat down on the driver's seat, unwrapped the reins from the driver's post.

It's all right, Johanna. Johanna?

He knew she thought he was going to hand her over to the Army. That this was probably an arranged meeting.

The man in front was a lieutenant; his shoulder insignia with the double bars winked in the dim light. Therefore it was a regular patrol trotting up and down the road on the south side of the Red looking for signs of raiders crossing over although with the flooding it was unlikely. They all carried the squareback Navy Colt five-shot revolvers that looked as big as pork hams in their holsters and the .56 caliber Colt carbines, also standard issue for the wild country.

The lieutenant called for the column to halt and then rode alongside and said, Good day. The ten men behind him kicked their feet out of the stirrups to relieve their knees and some took the opportunity to drink from canteens. At the rear their pack mules brayed at his horses in long demented shrieks like train whistles.

Good day, said the Captain.

The lieutenant looked over the wagon and saw the girl on the floor of the wagon bed just behind the Captain, her expression of stiffened fright, or even terror. She was as close to the Captain's revolver as she could get. She slid out her hand and grasped the butt where it lay hidden under the flitch of bacon, her hand and arm covered in the red wool serape.

The young lady seems very disturbed, said the lieutenant. There was surprise in his voice, suspicion.

She was a captive, said the Captain. I'm returning her to her people in Castroville, Bexar County. He handed over the Agent's papers.

I'd like to have a look at her, said the lieutenant. He read through the papers. The Agent's handwriting was very good, very clear. He read it easily, the girl's description, her approximate height and complexion. Then he raised his head. His shoulder bars winked with drops. The river made an endless thunder to their left. They could see it through the trees.

Yes, I'll try, said the Captain. He settled his hat more firmly on his head and stepped over the back of the wagon seat and grasped the thick red wool and pulled it from her head.

Johanna, he said. Johanna. He patted her shoulder.

Well damn, said the lieutenant. He was taken aback by the flat, wild look on the girl's face. You'd think she would be happy to be going home.

The Captain stood between Johanna and the lieutenant. He said, They took her at age six. As far as she knows she's a Kiowa.

I see. Well, I hope you'll apprise her of the facts. He leaned to one side to see around the Captain and stared at her appraisingly and then bent from his saddle to hand the papers back to the Captain. He said, You're the man who reads the news.

Yes, I am.

I was there at Fort Belknap when you read.

Glad to hear it.

I don't suppose you have your loyalty oath papers to show me.

No, I don't.

Since you are on a sort of official business you will need them. If you voluntarily aided the Confederate Army in any way you will need a certified copy of your loyalty oath.

I did not.

Were your boys in the conflict?

I don't have any.

Are you armed?

All I have is a twelve-gauge shotgun.

Let me see it.

Captain Kidd drew out the old shotgun and worked the bolt and caught the shell as it flew out. Bird shot. He stood in the wagon bed and handed it over. Johanna had in some way fed her thin body almost completely under the wagon seat and again drew up the thick red wool Mexican blanket over her head. She drew the revolver close to her and stared at the wagon floorboards and listened to every nuance, every tone in the men's voices. It was clear that the Captain was not going to let them have her. The Army man was a man with a hard voice but now his voice dropped and became more conversational.

How is it charged? the lieutenant said.

Number Seven bird shot.

Can't do much with that. I suppose it's all right. The lieutenant handed it back. You don't carry a rifle or a handgun?

Well hell no, said the Captain. He slid the shotgun back into the wagon bed. I might run into some Comanches and they'd take it away from me. He brought out his tobacco and filled his pipe. They might shoot me with it, he said. He struck a match.

There was no point in saying anything about the gaudy and corrupt Reconstruction government running Texas, the mindless law against carrying handguns, even up here on the frontier.

Johanna listened as the Captain's voice developed an edge. He was being insulting to the soldiers. Her eyes brightened.

Yes, very funny, said the lieutenant. He ran his eyes over everything in the wagon bed; the provisions and blankets, the little iron stove, the portfolio of newspapers, a sack of cornmeal, the sack of dimes and other coins, his shot box with the paper hulls and bird shot, a small keg of flour. He glanced at a flitch of bacon beside the wagon seat on the left side. The lieutenant regarded the flour keg and said, What's in that?

Flour.

Very well. I suspect they'll rescind that law here before long. I know people need sidearms to defend themselves.

Surely not, said the Captain.

The lieutenant ignored this. And you are going where?

Weatherford, Dallas, then south to Castroville and San Antonio.

Very well. A long way. Good day, sir. I wish you a safe trip.

SONS OF BITCHES, he said. You can come out now, Johanna. You can reappear like the flowers in May. They aren't going to slap you in leg irons and throw you into a cell. He smoked his pipe as he flicked the reins. The pipe had been carved from kaolin into the shape of a man's head and in the damp air the smoke hung unmoving so that they traveled on away from it and left it behind them hanging in the air. Johanna?

From behind him he heard, Kep-dun.

Don't stick a knife in my back. Don't let me hear the dreaded click of a cocked revolver hammer. Let us flounder on through life here as best we might.

Kep-dun!

She sprang lightly over the back of the driver's seat and sat down beside him. She held the revolver in one hand between her knees. She made several signs of which he only understood one, which was "good" and the other "let loose" or "free." Something like that. She smiled for the first time. There was no sign for "thank you." There was no word in Kiowa for "thank you." People should know that the one was grateful, because you know you have done something good, something commendable and there is no need to belabor the point. Kiowa is a tonal language and it sings up and down the complex verbs, and that by itself should be enough to express gratitude at being saved from the men in blue coats with the big long Army revolvers like hog's legs on their thighs, with their coats and pants all exactly the same, which was in itself unnatural. He had faced them down and saved her. She tilted her head to one side to regard him with a bright look on her small round face.

Yes, let loose, he said. Free. He carefully took the .38 from her hand, clicked on the safety, and returned it to the left side of the seat and put the flitch over it again. *She knew how to take the safety off,* he thought. He smiled back at her in a rather stiff grimace.

She wrestled with the yards of unfamiliar skirts and settled herself and smiled a small, slight smile at the sepia-toned, dripping world of the Red River valley. It was more a lift of the powdery blond eyebrows than a smile. She said something in Kiowa in a happy tone. *My name is Ay-ti-Podle, the Cicada, whose song means there is fruit ripening nearby.* She gestured back toward the big bay saddle horse and tossed her hair back. It was as if she wanted to include Pasha in this newfound happiness.

Ah, Cho-henna, he said. He turned and looked down at her. If the officer had reached for her he had no doubt she would have cocked the revolver and shot him point-blank.

He said, Your relatives are going to be so happy to get back their sweet precious lamb.

Kep-dun! she said, brightly, and patted his bony hand.

Cho-henna, he said.

SPANISH FORT WAS a mile from the river inside a great bend. The Red River was the boundary between Indian Territory and that which was not Indian Territory. They had passed through a tangled country of short, sharp hills with knobs of stone on top of them that stood like monuments, like curtain walls. As they went on toward Spanish Fort they passed them by at walking speed and stared at them as if watching distant castles. A storm rolled up out of the northern March sky, out of the plains.

They came to the town of Spanish Fort in the late afternoon. It was also known as Red River Station and with its two names it was busy. There had been at one time some sort of defensive works here, perhaps Spanish, perhaps not, but they were long gone. The Captain held the reins taut and dodged other vehicles. Johanna at first sat in the back, far inside the bulk of the Mexican-made *jorongo;* she clutched it tight around her so that she was the shape of a lime kiln in bright red and black.

The Captain's excursion wagon made sharp noises as the shafts turned on the fifth wheel beneath his feet. They locked wheels briefly with a freight wagon and it took the driver and the Captain and several bystanders to get them backed and free. Pasha sat back on his halter rope but didn't break it. By this time the Captain was red mud to the knees. Red mud crusted the laces on his old lace-up boots. The streets were filled with layers of wood smoke as supper was now in preparation in the houses and establishments of the town.

He turned his head to look up at second stories and at the people in the second stories doing what he could not tell other than arguing and slamming the windows shut against the wind. Horse soldiers rode by in twos. The wind came running at them from the northwest at full charge and blew off people's hats and tore at clotheslines. Town noises bit at the Captain's nerves and so what must it be like for her? He turned to pat her on the back, thudding gently on the thick red wool. She glanced up at him with fright on her face.

There was a great barn on the far edge of town that served as a place to park but it was full of every imaginable four-wheeled conveyance. Not far away was the U.S. Cavalry encampment, so he drove into a tight grove of bur oaks beyond the edge of the town. There he put up the overhead canopy and then one of the side curtains, and the other side curtain he stretched out as an awning over the tailgate. He belled Fancy and then hobbled both her and Pasha and set them loose to graze. He stood for a moment to watch Pasha, with his thick, curved neck and large eyes. He was both smooth and calm. He remembered seeing the horse in a lot of twenty to be sold in Dallas. He had instantly turned away because if the dealer had seen the look on his face the price would have gone up a hundred dollars.

Finally the Captain went to heave out the flour keg. He took out the box of .38 shells and put it under the seat.

Everything good, he said to Johanna. He beat the flour from his hands. Here, my dear, do something. Try to get this stove going.

Yes, Kep-dun, yes yes.

She darted under the oaks, still barefoot, to gather firewood. Lightning cracked overhead with a noise like artillery while its blinding neurons of fire ran to every quarter of the sky. Spanish Fort was busy with freight wagons and supply establishments, with longhorn herds milling outside the town waiting to cross and anxious men conferring under canvas as to when the flood would subside. Trying to figure out how to get them over the Red before they ate up all the grass on this side of the river and starved.

SIX

———◦•◦———

CAPTAIN KIDD LEFT her feeding sticks into the toylike cast-iron stove and walked back into town grasping his hat brim. He found the man who took care of the Masonic Lodge and arranged to rent it that night. Then he walked about town to put up his bills. If he did not have the girl to care for he would not have to stay at the wagon, he could rent a room with a kerosene lamp and curtains and take a bath and he could eat in a restaurant. God above knew what she would do if presented with a dinner on a plate. In the light mist he tacked up each notice with four tacks. He had learned long ago that anything less left his advertisements prey to the wind and they invariably ended up in the hands of people who needed the paper to write grocery lists on, or for other purposes.

He came upon a fiddler he knew. Simon Boudlin sat behind the glass window of a storefront that was both a ladies' millinery and a meat market. Simon sat in the window with his chin on his fist and his fiddle under one arm as if he were a display. He was watching the world go by. He was a short man but he carried himself as if he were six feet tall; he had straight, broad, and perfectly square shoulders and slim hips. His thick hair was a halo of unruly brown burrs, and he was freckled as a guinea egg. Simon lifted his fiddle bow by the frog and tapped on the glass. Captain Kidd saw him and went in.

Simon.

Captain.

Are you playing tonight? Because I am reading.

Where?

At the Masonic Lodge.

The Captain joined Simon in the window on another chair and laid his tack hammer and the sheaf of advertisements on the floor. He wiped off his old field hat with his sleeve.

No, it's all right, said Simon. I have already played. No competition. He smiled. He had two teeth broken out of his jaw on the left side but you couldn't see it unless he smiled and then deep parentheses formed on either side of his mouth. He worked sometimes for the wheelwright and a wheel had come off the lathe where they were boring out the hub box and struck him in the jaw. Why are you here? He was not talkative until he had something to say. He was a careful listener and cocked his head like a titmouse, which he did now. Raindrops slid and sparkled on the glass and beyond it people wavered past with their heads down.

I am on my way to Dallas and then on south, said the Captain. Coming from Wichita Falls.

You got across the Little Wichita, then.

Yes, and I think so did Britt Johnson and his crew. They went straight south. So you have nothing to do?

Simon shook his head. I just played for the Fort Worth

Dancing School master. They had the dancing school in the back, here. He pointed with the bow. The fellow who was supposed to play guitar for them was tuning his guitar there at the church on the piano and he got it an octave too high and busted every one of his strings. Simon bent his head down and laughed. Bang bang bang one after the other, you'd think he would have figured it out. He wiped his hand down his face to stop himself from laughing at the guitar player's misfortunes. Well, well, I did it myself once, long ago. And so! They came and got me out of the wheelwright's to play for them. You see. He plucked a curled shaving from his pants leg.

Well then, listen. Captain Kidd shifted from one foot to another and briefly wondered if Johanna might have already absconded into the woods. He regarded his boots. His pants. Mud to the shins. Several women were buying ground meat, a man churned it out of a big-spouted grinder in a red sludge. On the other side of the store a girl and her friend were trying on hats. From the rear of the store came the light voices of yet more girls and the sound of several young men whose voices were very low and at other times broke and vaulted up the register. They came filing out carrying their dancing slippers. The Captain lifted his hat to them. Listen, he said. He groped around in his head for sentences and phrases and words to explain the situation.

I'm listening, I'm listening, said the fiddler. He lightly tapped the head of the bow on the floor between his feet. Some song was running through his head.

The thing is, I am returning a girl who was a Kiowa captive to her people, down south near San Antonio, and she's in the wagon there, in that bur oak stand behind the livery barn, cooking dinner in my wagon.

Simon looked out the rainy glass at the vehicles passing by, the men and women hurrying along the raw, new boardwalk.

You jest, he said. That's four hundred miles.

No, I do not.

How old is she?

Ten. But Simon, she is wise in the ways of battle and conflict, it seems to me.

Simon watched a cowboy walk by with his hat slanted against the increasing rain and his boots shining with wet.

The fiddler nodded and said, They are always at war.

Be that as it may. She has lost all acquaintance with the uses and manners of white people and I need somebody to keep watch on her while I do my reading. You and your particular friend Miss Dillon would do me a great favor if you would sit with her while I read. I am afraid if I left her alone she might go bolting off.

Simon nodded slowly like a walking beam. He thought about it.

She wants to go back to them, he said.

She apparently does.

I know of a person who was like that, said Simon. They called him Kiowa Dutch. He was blond-haired completely. Nobody knew where he had been captured from, or when. He didn't either. I played for a dance there at Belknap when they brought him in. He got away from the Army fellows who were returning him and he is up there yet.

I think I heard about him, said the Captain. He drummed his fingers on his knee. You know, it is chilling, how their minds change so completely. But I have taken on this task and I have to try.

Simon lifted his fiddle and ran the bow across the strings. His fingers, hard and coarse with joinery work, blunt at the tips, skipped on the strings and a tune emerged: "Virginia Belle." *She bereft us when she left us, sweet Virginia Belle.* Then he stopped and said, Sorry. I can't help it. So yes. I will go and get Doris. He sat for a moment considering where Doris might be. Probably attending a lady named Everetson who was ill with a fever. A yawn overtook him and he lifted the back of the fiddle over his mouth the way nonfiddlers would cover a yawn with their hand. He said, Captain, you have taken on a heavy load here, I'm afraid. He tapped his fiddle bow on his shoe.

For an old man is what you mean.

Simon stood and then bent to his case, flipped a piece of waxed silk around his instrument, and laid it in the velvet. Click click he snapped the catches shut. He straightened.

Yes, for an old man is what I mean exactly.

THE CAPTAIN AND Simon and Doris all hurried through the drizzle to the stand of bur oaks. Between their overhead of rust-colored leaves and the canopy and stretched side curtains, the wagon was dry enough. The girl had made them a supper of corn-bread and bacon and coffee and was sitting cross-legged between the long seats like a Hindu yoga with it spread before her. In the lantern light the gold letters of *Curative Waters* shone brightly.

They ducked under the side-curtain awning.

Doris pulled off her dripping straw hat and said, Hello!

Johanna glanced at the Captain as if to ask if he, too, saw this female apparition and then returned her gaze to Doris without saying a word.

Doris carried a small bundle. She unwrapped it and held it out to the girl with a bright smile. It was a doll with a china head and painted dark eyes. It wore a dress in a brown and green check and shawl and its shoes were painted black on china feet. Johanna reached out one dirty hand from under her blanket and took the doll by the foot. She held it around the body for a moment. It was like the *taina* sacred figure that was taken from its wrappings only at the Sun Dance. She looked searchingly into its eyes. Then she propped it against one of the side benches and opened both her hands to it and said something in Kiowa.

Hmm, said Simon. He stood under the stretched canvas and tousled his hair to shake off the wet. He had left his fiddle safe in his tiny room over the wagon maker's. He wore an old 1840s infantry coat with a high band collar. Its surface was a series of patches, some of which overlapped. My word. I believe she is *addressing* it. The fiddler held out his hands to the heat of the little stove, and worked his stiff fingers open and shut to loosen the joints.

Doris found the ironstone plates in the cook box. She said, she is like an elf. She is like a fairy person from the *glamorie*. They are not one thing or another. She laid out the plates wherever she could find room on the tailgate and on tops of boxes.

Simon regarded the light of his life with a solemn expression. Doris, he said, your Irish comes out at the strangest times.

Don't stare at her, said Doris. That is what she is.

She thinks it's an idol, said Simon. The Captain bent over the tailgate searching through his carpetbag and listened to them.

Aye, perhaps, said Doris. She shoveled food onto the plates and laid whatever utensil she could find on each one; the two forks, the camp knife, a serving spoon and then lifted her head to look at the girl; so alone, twice captured, carried away on the flood of the world. Doris's eyes burned suddenly with tears and she lifted the back of her hand to her eyes. But I think not. The doll is like herself, not real and not not-real. I make myself understood I hope. You can put her in any clothing and she remains as strange as she was before because she has been through two creations. Doris laid a plate before the girl. Doris's hair was Irish black with blue lights in it, a rare, true black. She was a small woman and her wrists were ropy with muscle and hard work. She said, To go through our first creation is a turning of the soul we hope toward the light, out of the animal world. God be with us. To go through another tears all the making of the first creation and sometimes it falls to bits. We fall into pieces. She is asking, Where is that rock of my creation?

The Captain took out shaving gear. He went to the far side and hung his mirror on a bolt end and shaved. He said, Miss Dillon, you know this how?

An Gorta Mor, she said. In the famine children saw their parents die and then went to live with the people on the other side. In their minds they went. When they came back they were unfinished. They are forever falling. She shook out her wet, pinned-up skirt and watched as Johanna carefully ate pieces of bacon with her hands.

Well, I don't know what I can do about it. The Captain came back around, put away his gear, and sat on the flour keg. He bent his long, elderly body with a light creaking of the spine and went through his newspapers. He had to make a living. This was intriguing but first he needed to hear the coins falling into the paint can; then he could listen to mysteries about unfinished children, trailing their griefs and ragged edges.

And the newspapers, they say nothing about this at all or about the poor at all, Doris said. There are great holes in your newspapers. Nobody sees them. God sees them.

The Captain ate his supper and then crossed his knife and fork on his plate and put the plate on the tailgate. Yes, I am sure He does. At any rate, she has to go back to her family. It's only my concern between here and Castroville.

Who are her people?

Germans.

Ah! Doris clapped both hands over her face for a moment and then dropped them in her lap. And so now that's three languages the child must know. She wiped her hands on flour sacking. Leave her with us, Captain. We will take her.

Simon stopped eating. He drew in his lower lip and raised both eyebrows in an expression of surprise.

Doris said, She is like my little sister that died.

Ahem, Doris, my dear, said Simon. And so we will be married next month with a child already.

Doris lifted her slim shoulders. The priest, she said, has seen everything.

The Captain thought, *The girl is trouble and contention wherever she goes, wherever she lands. No one wants her for herself. A redheaded stepchild destined for the washhouse.*

Miss Dillon, that is generous of you but I must return her to her relatives as I said I would do, and for which I took a coin of fifty dollars in gold.

Simon's relief was plain in his face.

The girl shrank away into the interior, against the backrest, and hid in the thick *jorongo*.

SEVEN

———•◦•———

CAPTAIN KIDD HAD changed into his reading clothes in the back of the Masonic Hall. They were a decent black frock coat, knee length, single-breasted, a matching vest, a white shirt in silk and cotton figured with a lyre design in silk of the same color—that is, a bit yellowed. He had one of the new ascots in black silk and a low-rise rounded silk topper. He stuffed his stained traveling clothes into the carpetbag and then went out and stepped up on the dais. He placed his bull's-eye lantern to the left on a wooden box (it said *Kilmeyer Beer 50 bttls*), so it would shine on his newspapers.

He greeted the crowd and listened to the clink of dimes and five-cent pieces, two-cent pieces, pennies, and sometimes quarters into the paint can and if it was a quarter people made their own change. There were a good plenty of people. Mist was still coming down in minute blowing drops from the clouds that raced through the sky over Spanish Fort. He unfolded the *London Daily News.* He would give them a few paragraphs of hard news and then read of dreamlike places far removed. This was the arrangement of all his readings. It worked. The lantern

beam shone sideways onto his face, casting brilliant lunar cells
of light on his cheekbones through the lenses of his reading
glasses. He read an article concerning the Franco-Prussian
War. It involved delicate Frenchmen, scented with toilet water,
being whipped soundly at Wissembourg by huge blond Germans who were fat and strong on sausages. The outcome was
easily predicted. The audience sat rapt, listening. News all the
way from France! Nobody knew anything about the Franco-
Prussian War but all were jointly amazed by information that
had come across the Atlantic to them, here in North Texas, to
their town alongside the flooding Red River. They had no idea
how it had got here, through what strange lands it had traveled,
who had carried it. Why.

Captain Kidd read carefully and precisely. His eyeglasses
were round and rimmed in gold over his deep eyes. He always
laid his small gold hunting watch to one side of the podium to
time his reading. He had the appearance of wisdom and age
and authority, which was why his readings were popular and
the reason the dimes rang into the coffee can. When they read
his handbills men abandoned the saloon, they slipped out of
various unnamed establishments, they ran through the rain
from their firelit homes, they left the cattle circled and bedded
beside the flooding Red to come and hear the news of the distant world.

And now he took them away to far places and strange
peoples. Into mythic forms of thought and the structures of
fairy tales. He read from the *Philadelphia Inquirer* of Dr.
Schliemann's search for windy Troy somewhere in Turkey.
He read of the telegraph wires successfully laid from Britain to

India, an article in the *Calcutta Times* forwarded to the London *Daily Telegraph,* a technological advance that seemed almost otherworldly. As he glanced up it seemed to the Captain that he saw the blond man again or at least the glint of ash-blond hair just at the borders of his light. This went into his mind and then out of his mind as he grappled with the big four-sheets of the *Boston Daily Journal.* To finish, he read of the unfortunate *Hansa* crushed in the pack ice in its attempt on the North Pole, the survivors rescued by a whaler. This was proving the most popular as he could see by the small gestures of the audience; they bent forward, they fixed their eyes upon him to hear of undiscovered lands in the kingdoms of ice, fabulous beasts, perils overcome, snow people in furry suits.

Simon came in the rear door of the Masonic Lodge just as he was replacing his newspapers into the portfolio.

Sir, the girl's gone.

Nothing galvanizes people like news of a missing child. The Captain swept everything into his portfolio, his newspapers and eyeglasses, the bull's-eye lantern with its smoldering wick, and the money tin; jammed his silk hat on his head; and ran to the door and straight out into the rain.

They had fallen asleep, he and Doris, sitting on the shot box and the flour keg, leaning together against the big rear wheel in front of a good fire. Something made Simon wake up and she was gone.

She had left on foot. The doll was gone too.

It is easier to track a barefoot person than somebody with shoes. The toes dig in with four distinct marks and the big toe like a misplaced thumb broad alongside. The bull's-eye lantern beam picked up her prints on the sloppy, red-clay road going out of Spanish Fort, east toward the river. The river which was joyous in its escape from banks and boundaries, which had become a rolling inland sea. They could hear it from half a mile away. The rain increased, lightning came cracking down out of the northwest as the new storm front moved in on them in the night. The lantern lit the million billion drops that came down in colors of steel and ice. She had followed the ruts in the wagon road that led to the river. The track wound about among the post oak and bur oaks, twisted trees with fright wigs of dry leaves and soon the track would come to the edge of the flood.

The Captain walked bent over and rained upon. His joints hurt. He needed to find somebody younger to take her south and deal with this kind of thing. Somebody agile and patient and strong.

He and Simon the fiddler soldiered on.

She's gone and it's my fault! Simon slapped himself on the thigh. It made a wet smack. Captain, I am so sorry!

He had to shout over the noise of the rain. He gripped his hat brim and ran alongside the Captain.

Never mind! the Captain shouted back. Can't be helped!

He would as soon have Simon with him as anybody. Despite his short stature the fiddler was very strong and a hard fighter and a good shot. They ran on into the rain as if into a thicket. They bulled their way through. They tripped over the cut stumps where someone had cleared ground and tangled themselves in the parasitic love vine. They came upon Pasha and Fancy grazing, and were snorted at. The Captain felt himself growing thinner even as they walked. A man his age should have more weight on him, he should be in a hotel room in Spanish Fort after a good supper and leaning on the sill with tobacco smoke rolling out of his nose, watching the dim lights in the windows and counting his money. This was unfair.

They stopped when they saw the glinting water. There at its edge, on a lift of red stone no more than thirty yards ahead, stood Johanna, wet as a dishcloth and her skirts heavy with rain. She clutched the doll to her chest. In the explosive lightning flashes the Captain could see, on the far side of the flood, a party of Indians. They were on the move. They had probably been flooded out of their campsite. The Red was still rising. Entire pecan trees rolled and ground like mill wheels in the current. The Indians had stopped to look across, perhaps at the distant lights of Spanish Fort, and Johanna was calling to them in Kiowa but they could not hear her. It was too far, the river was too loud.

Johanna! the Captain called. Johanna!

She put down the doll and shouted at the Indians with her hands around her mouth. What could she possibly think would happen? That they would come for her? She was shouting for her mother, for her father and her sisters and brothers, for the life on the Plains, traveling wherever the buffalo took them, she was calling for her people who followed water, lived with every contingency, were brave in the face of enemies, who could go without food or water or money or shoes or hats and did not care that they had neither mattresses nor chairs nor oil lamps. They stood and stared across the water at her like creatures of the *sidhe*, wet and shining in every flash from overhead. They stood among their jackstrawed tipi poles heaped on horses, drenched children gazing at her out of buffalo robes on the travois, the men ahead and at the side with their weapons wrapped in whatever would keep them dry. One of them shouted back over the water. The lightning made them appear in every detail like an intaglio and then disappear and then reappear again.

Johanna called again. *I have been taken prisoner, rescue me, take me back.* She would turn her back on the modern world with the telegraph and the railroads and its elaborate political constructions piled layer upon layer. Everything gone . . . everything. And she would live in constant movement over the face of the earth, in gratitude to the sun and the grass, often dirty and lousy and wet and cold like those on the other side but she did not care.

One of the warriors on the far side unsheathed a long weapon and lifted it. A lengthy barrel shone blue-white in a lightning flash. He aimed it and fired. A muzzle flash as long as a chimney brush and then the heavy bullet struck the stone near them and sent pieces of red sandstone flying. The report came to them as a dull *chunk* sound. They had not heard her; they didn't know who she was. A warning shot; stay away.

The fiddler and the Captain fell flat, hands outstretched in the tall brown grasses.

That was a Sharps! shouted the fiddler.

The girl still called out, she had not moved. Then she bent to place the doll to sit against the rock, facing Indian Territory.

Fifty caliber, said the Captain. If he fired once he'll fire again.

He jumped up and grabbed the ten-year-old girl by the back of her dress and swung her around and ran. He shifted his grasp to one of her arms, and the fiddler got the other arm and so they dragged her back to her fate. To the wagon, to the white man's necessary world which did not seem to want her either. Another giant five-hundred-and-twenty-grain bullet tore through the air overhead. Even above the noise of the rain they heard the *nyow-ow-ow* sound and it hit a bur oak and tore off a limb big as a drainpipe.

At the *Curative Waters* wagon the Captain sat awake late in the rainy dark and counted his money and thought about the long series of roads to San Antonio and Castroville. The girl was asleep. He slowly changed his clothes. He hurt in all his joints. He reflected on how she had not cried once. His pipe and the tot of rum Doris and Simon had left for him were of some comfort. He needed it. He stewed silently at the imposition of it all. He must have been out of his mind. Senile dementia. But he had promised. *I'll do it,* he thought. *I will get her back to her relatives if I never cock another gun.* He read through the Boston paper, staring mindlessly at advertisements for cures and false hair.

THEY CONTINUED ON to the south. He had forgotten to find a blacksmith for the cracked tire rim but the wheels had swollen in the wet and perhaps had seized it tight to the felloes. The trace chains jingled, the horses' hooves kicked up little gouts of mud, the forested, hilly landscape slowly moved backward on either side. It was a mild day with white steam rising from the damp hollows. He would have to get the tire fixed in Dallas and his money was short. After he had paid the Masonic Hall and bought more supplies and grain for the horses, there was not much left.

Since they had left the town she now sat up beside him and sang to herself, one hand dancing in the air. With the resilience of a ten-year-old she had accepted that she could not cross the Red and rejoin her people and so she sang and made dancing gestures.

Well then, Johanna, he said. He had calmed himself. It was time to be patient. Auntie? Uncle? You will soon see them.

She stared straight ahead with the blank look that meant a dredging of the mind, a searching through old indexes.

He tried German. *Tante* Anna, he said. *Onkle* Vilhelm.

She turned to him. *Ja,* she said. There was surprise in her voice. Then she seemed to struggle with a tangled thing inside her head, something knotted that would not unknot.

She opened both stained hands on her lap and stared at the palms. She shut her fingers. She wasn't really seeing anything. Her face was no longer a child's face but one that had gone through something beyond description or comprehension and so was suspended for a moment in wordlessness. Her hands opened and shut, opened and shut.

And then she spoke. Mama, Papa. She lifted her head to him. *Todt,* she said.

They rolled through a bur oak forest with the steady click of the break in the iron tire counting out its revolutions; Fancy's harness jingled. Crooked zigzag limbs sifted through the air. Beneath them the crisp shells of acorns made crushed sounds.

The Captain looked down at her, into her guileless eyes and the rediscovered pain in them. Sudden terrible memories. He bit the left side of his lower lip and was sorry he had brought it up. He tucked the blanket more tightly around her neck and smiled at her.

He said, Never mind, my dear. Let's try an English lesson. She nodded gravely with one hand opening and shutting on a sleeve flounce.

Hand, he said. He held up his hand.

Hont, she said.

Horse. He pointed to Fancy jogging along ahead of them.

Hoas.

The Captain knew nothing of the Kiowa language but he knew it had no *R*.

Very good! he said in a cheerful tone.

Felly good.

But now her voice was low and discouraged. She had left the *taina* to keep watch across the Red River for her. That was taken care of. Now she had to begin a new, long, hard road to somewhere else. Felly good.

THEY CROSSED CLEAR Creek and then Denton Creek and two days later they came finally into the small town of Dallas about four o'clock of a chilly afternoon. The girl was even more subdued and frightened than in Spanish Fort, stunned by the noise and the wagons. There were several two-story buildings of brick and stone. She jumped back into the rear and pressed against the backrest of the wagon seat, between the flour keg and his carpetbag. They came in to town on the north road, where it led past several blacksmith shops with their great shed-roof caverns and lit with scarlet light, full of men and horses, tobacco smoke and the noise of metal being forced to hold the things of this world together bolt by bolt. Johanna glanced into them with deep apprehension. The Captain was happy to see them. He would bring the wagon in tomorrow. First, of course, he would have to ask the price of a new tire rim and the labor.

On into town, down Trinity Street, full of white men wearing their tight-fitting clothing and women in dresses that were architectural constructions of cloth and whalebone. Johanna gazed with some interest at two black women carrying shopping baskets with the heads of alarmed hens sticking out. Finally the Captain came into Gannet's livery stable yard and there stepped down.

The stableman took hold of Fancy's driving bridle and cried, Whoa there! As if the weary little roan were about to charge through the back end of the fairway.

Hang on to her there, said the Captain. She's about to go completely wild on you.

Fancy hung her head and rolled her tongue under the straight bar of the driving bit and then yawned.

Never know, the man said. Unpredictable, new horse, never saw it before. He hiccupped.

Yes, said the Captain. You must only see new horses three or four times a day.

The man unhitched the little roan and took the harness from her back. The Captain could smell alcohol on the man's breath.

Mrs. Gannet came out of the feed storage room with three empty flowered feed sacks in her hands. Her bonnet sat on the back of her head and the strings hung down over her shoulders. Still very trim, the Captain thought. Girlish waist.

Captain Kidd! she cried. She smiled and came to stand with one hand on the *Curative Waters* wagon's side to see the girl staring out of the red wool with eyes like a carp. She turned to the Captain with an interrogative look. As he explained he stood at the high back wheel with one arm on it, taller than Mrs. Gannet by a head. Even as he told his story he wondered that she ran the livery stable by herself. He was worn and stained with Red River sludge and he had to go about buying newspapers in what he stood up in. No help for it.

San Antonio! said Mrs. Gannet. God above. That is very far, Captain. And you'll be alone on the roads. There's news of more raids all through the country. She turned to the stableman to see what he was doing. The Captain knew that raids were how she had become a widow. A year ago they had found Mr. Gannet in several pieces along the Weatherford road and none of them had any clothes on them. She said, Wait for a convoy, will you not?

Yes, yes, he said. We'll see. It will be all right. He saw her dubious expression. I'm armed, he said. A sidearm and a shotgun. And now I have to go find the latest newspapers and a hotel. May I leave her with you for a few hours? I don't think she'll run away and go flitting about Dallas. In Spanish Fort there was someplace to go. The river. Here, she's deep inside enemy territory so to speak. He ran his blue-veined hand over a two-day growth of silver grizzle. I'm a mess, Mrs. Gannet.

She laughed and said for the Captain to go about his business, she could look after the girl. If he would care to change in the feed room she would send out his traveling clothes to Mrs. Carnahan and also she would ask Mrs. Carnahan if she had a secondhand dress to fit the girl and perhaps other necessary garments. The girl needed a change of clothing. He reached for his portfolio and looked down at her. Widowed, no more than forty-five. Painfully young. She had eyes of a leaf-colored hazel and a good smile.

I am very grateful, the Captain said. He lifted his hat to her, replaced it. I will settle up when we leave tomorrow.

He turned to Johanna and was surprised when her small hand appeared out of the *jorongo* and reached for his. She was very frightened and perhaps thought she was to be handed over to yet another stranger. He smiled and put his hand on her forehead, briefly, in lieu of patting her cheek, which was hidden behind the red wool.

It's all right, he said. It's all right.

He took out his hunting watch. Then he put it back. Johanna had no idea of time. It was pointless to tell her he would be back in an hour. So he just said,

Sit. Stay.

EIGHT

————•◦•————

THE CAPTAIN CHANGED, left his traveling clothes with Mrs. Gannet, and went back out onto the street. He took his portfolio of newpapers under his arm and then engaged two rooms in a hotel on Stemmons Ferry Road; it was a balloon-frame building with thin walls and flowered grain sacks for curtains but he was as yet unsure how much money he would make from his reading. Baths were fifty cents, an outrageous price, but he paid it and sat for fifteen minutes in the hot water and then shaved.

He found the proprietor of the Broadway Playhouse sitting in the Bluebonnet Saloon having an early drink and engaged the small theater for the night. He wrote it down and had the man sign it in case he got too drunk and forgot.

He went on down Trinity to Thurber's News and Printing Establishment where he was greeted and seduced by the smell of ink and the noise of the press coming from the rear. It was a Chandler and Price hand-fed paten press, slowly chunking out page after page of announcements or advertising. All around were sticks of type and the bindery equipment, the perforating machine. A sign on the wall:

THIS IS
A PRINTING OFFICE

CROSSROADS OF CIVILIZATION

Refuge of all the arts against the ravages of time

ARMOURY OF FEARLESS TRUTH

AGAINST WHISPERING RUMOR

INCESSANT TRUMPET OF TRADE

From this place words may fly abroad

NOT TO PERISH ON WAVES OF SOUND

NOT TO VARY WITH THE WRITER'S HAND

BUT FIXED IN TIME HAVING BEEN VERIFIED
IN PROOF

Friend you stand on sacred ground

THIS IS A PRINTING OFFICE

The Captain took a deep breath to subdue the sudden bitter slash of envy and then felt more or less all right. Thurber greeted him and inquired after his health, his readings, his journeys, and the Indian threat from the north. Did he not find traveling onerous? The Captain fixed Thurber with his dark eyes and said no, he did not, and assured him that he, Jefferson Kyle Kidd, had not yet been forced to confine himself to a bath chair or an invalid's bed and when he did he would notify Thurber with a postcard. Thank you, sir, for your concern.

The Captain stalked around the print shop and gazed at the layout tables and type cases. Thurber clasped his hands behind his back and rolled his eyes at his two printer's devils. Then the Captain bought a sheet of letter paper and an envelope, and the latest editions of the *Philadelphia Inquirer* and the *Chicago Tribune,* the *London Times,* the *New-York Herald,* and *El Clarion,* a Mexico City newspaper. He would sit at peace in the hotel room, under a proper roof, and find articles of interest in the English-language papers and then translate some articles from *El Clarion.*

Then he went down Trinity to the *Dallas Weekly Courier* offices, much refreshed from having snarled at Thurber, to sit with their Morse operator and take news from the AP wire. The fee was reasonable. The wire from Arkansas and points east was still operating. The Comanche and Kiowa had learned to cut the wire and then repair it with horsehair so that it would not transmit but no one could tell where it had been cut. They well knew Army orders came over the telegraph wires.

He took out the thick sheaf of printed notices and handbills from his portfolio and, there in the *Courier* offices, inked in the last line.

THE
LATEST NEWS AND ARTICLES
FROM THE MAJOR JOURNALS
OF THE CIVILIZED WORLD
CAPTAIN JEFFERSON KYLE KIDD
WILL READ A COMPENDIUM
FROM SELECTED NEWSPAPERS AT 8:00 P.M.
AT THE BROADWAY PLAYHOUSE

He walked around the streets of Dallas tacking up his notices as he went. These small towns in North Texas were always hungry for news and for a presenter to read it. It was so much more entertaining than sitting at home reading the papers, having only yourself or your spouse to whom you could make noises of outrage or astonishment. Then, of course, there were those who could not read at all or only haltingly.

He worried all up and down every street and with every tack he drove in. Worried about the very long journey ahead, about his ability to keep the girl from harm. He thought, resentfully, *I raised my girls. I already did that.* At the age he had attained with his life span short before him he had begun to look upon the human world with the indifference of a condemned man. *Who cares for your fashions and your wars and your causes? I will shortly be gone and I have seen many fashions come and go and many causes so passionately defended only to be forgotten.* But now it was different and he was drawn back into the stream of being because there was once again a life in his hands. Things mattered. The strange depression and spiritual chill he had felt back in Wichita Falls was gone. But still he objected. He was an old man. A cranky old man. *I raised two of them already.* A celestial voice said, *Well then, do it again.* The Captain had to admit that this was his own inner voice, which always sounded something like that of his father, the magistrate, who had often recalled to his son the law under the Crown, in Colonial North Carolina, his voice speculative and gentle and lightly agreeable with drink.

THE COOL SPRING wind skipped from roof to roof and dived down into the streets and flung women's hems up in rolling loops. The Captain could see his breath. He pulled the tattered muffler close around his throat and shoved his good black hat down over his white hair. Texas weather was changeable as the moon. He bought barbecue and bread and a dish of sodden, unhappy-looking squash and carried it all back to the livery stable stacked in a tin pail.

Kep-dun! He heard her voice in a loud happy cry.

Yes, Johanna, he said.

Mrs. Gannet looked over the edge of a box stall with her bright hazel eyes and wide smile. He could just see the top of Johanna's head. Mrs. Gannet told him all was well, that the girl took some comfort in the horses, and that they were learning all their names. The Captain found this a relief. His new-washed traveling trousers and two old shirts had been hung to dry over the wagon's dashboard and his socks and unmentionables discreetly steamed, still hot from the tub, on the tie-rods beneath. The girl's new secondhand clothing had been packed in the ammunition box.

He opened the dinner pail on the lowered tailgate. Mrs. Gannet went back into her office. The Captain watched her go. A strand of her dark brown hair had fallen from the confines of her bonnet and her dress skirt moved very nicely without hoops.

Then he turned to Johanna.

Dinner, he said, carefully.

Dinnah! The girl smiled and showed all her row of bottom teeth and gathered up her skirts to climb a wheel by the spokes into the wagon.

He and Johanna sat on the side seats and he watched as she took the camp butcher knife to cut off a great piece of the smoking barbecued meat, tossed it from hand to hand crying Ah!

Ah! and when it was cool tossed it expertly into her mouth. Barbecue sauce flew. The Captain paused with his fork halfway to his mouth and watched her. She cut another piece and began tossing it; her fingers were slick with fat and there was red barbecue sauce up to her wrists.

Stop.

He put down his fork and wiped her hands with the napkins that had come with the dinner and placed the fork in her hands. He grasped her small fingers, fork and all, in his bony and veined hand and pushed the tines into the brisket and then lifted it to her mouth.

She regarded him with that flat and vitreous stare that meant, he had learned, that she neither understood nor liked what she was seeing. She took the fork as one would grasp an ice pick and stabbed it into her dinner. She wrenched a piece loose and ate it from the tines.

No, my dear, he said. He put his hand over hers, once again placed the fork correctly, and once again lifted it to her mouth. Then he sat on his own side of the wagon and saw her struggling with the fork, the knife, the stupidity of it, the unknown reasons that human beings would approach food in this manner, reasons incomprehensible, inexplicable, for which they had no common language. She tried again, and then turned and threw the fork into a box stall.

The Captain's shoulders dropped a fraction of an inch under his black formal coat. He was suddenly almost overwhelmed with pity for her. Torn from her parents, adopted by a strange culture, given new parents, then sold for a few blankets and some old silverware, now sent to stranger after stranger, crushed into peculiar clothing, surrounded by people of an un-known language and an unknown culture, only ten years old, and now she could not even eat her food without having to use outlandish instruments.

Finally he took his satchel in one hand, tucked his portfo-lio under his arm, and beckoned to Johanna. He saw her look down at her stained hands and there were tears on her cheeks.

We're going to try to get you into a hotel room, he said in a firm voice. And you are going to have to stay there without breaking out the windows while I prepare my reading.

He took hold of her greasy small hand and they started off down the street.

NINE

———

THE CAPTAIN WENT out and locked the hotel room door behind him. He stood in the hallway. He could hear her begin a Kiowa chant. This could mean anything. It could mean she was resigned, it could mean she was going to hang herself with the curtain cording, or set the place on fire, or go to sleep.

At least she didn't have a weapon.

At the desk he laid down the key and said, She was a Kiowa captive. I am returning her.

But Captain! You'd think she'd be happy! The young man at the desk had protuberant eyes and in his hands was a false mustache. He was shaping it with a pair of nail scissors. You'd think she'd be skipping about and clapping her hands! That sounds like she is about to stab herself! It's operatic!

I know, said the Captain.

Where is she going?

To near San Antonio.

You mean you are putting up with that all the way to San Antonio? Perish and forbid!

Young man, stop speaking in exclamation points. I have no idea what to do about it.

The desk clerk breathed out, long and carefully, with his eyes closed. He often played bit parts at the playhouse, usually a page or a messenger. He said, Go get Mrs. Gannet to stay with her. We can't listen to this all night.

THE CAPTAIN SAW that Mrs. Gannet had quite a lot of rich brown hair knotted in complex braids coiled all around her head. She had taken off her bonnet to beat it on a stall rail to knock the dust off. She was instructing the stableman in a method of removing Chicago screws from a bridle.

Yes ma'am! he said, and turned and crossed one leg over another and fell down. Well Billy be-goddamn bangtree, he said. Legs, floor, unexpected. His words were slurred.

Peter, she said. You are swearing. Get up.

Things! he said. Under hay. Trip a person.

Well then, pick them up, she said, gently. Yes, Captain? She tried to smile.

The Captain stood formally with his hands crossed in front of him. He asked her to come and stay the night with Johanna but did not, of course, mention the other reason, which was that it would be delightful, yes, enchanting to think of her sleeping in the room next to his. He offered her a dollar to compensate.

Captain, *please*, she said. I am delighted to help.

That evening was the first time in the last week he could, he hoped, rest without cares, without tension and fear. Fear that the girl would run away and be lost and die of hunger, would try to swim the Red to get back to her Kiowa family. For the first two days he had wondered if she might attempt to kill him. Or herself.

Mrs. Gannet had come prepared to spend the entire night with her nightgown and other articles in a small brass-clasped thing that looked like a green fabric saddlebag. He opened the door to the room where Johanna sat on the floor cross-legged, rocking herself. Mrs. Gannet drew a light and delicate piece of divinity from her jacket pocket and held it out. Johanna fixed her blank stare on it. The Captain saw her make the sign for "poison."

He said, Eat half of it, Mrs. Gannet.

She understood immediately and bit half of the white candy and said, Mmmmm!

Johanna reached up and took the other half from her in a glacially slow movement and bit down on the taste of vanilla and sugar and egg white, felt the light crinkling of divinity shell in her mouth. She ate it unsmiling. The Captain knew Mrs. Gannet had made it that afternoon, for Johanna. Divinity was very difficult to make. He backed out slowly and heard the lock click to.

The walls of the hotel were made of cheap deal board and he could hear everything from the room next door and wished he could not. He sat down to outline his articles in ink, his pen nib scratching across the rough newsprint with a noise like avaricious mice. He blew on the ink and then laid the newspapers aside and took up the letter paper to write to his daughters in Georgia. The room smelled of new, raw lumber and the harsh soap they had used to wash the quilts and sheets.

My dearest daughters Olympia and Elizabeth, he wrote.

Kep-dun! Johanna banged on the wall. She was sobbing. He banged back. Cho-henna, he said.

My greetings and constant love to Emory and my grandchildren. I am well and continue to make my rounds with the news of the day and as always am well-received in the towns of which we have more than a few now as the Century grows older and the population increases so that large crowds come to hear reportage of distant places as well as those nearby. I enjoy good health as always and hope that Emory is doing well using his left hand now and look forward to an example of his handwriting. It is true what Elizabeth has said about employment for a one-armed man but that concerns manual labor only and at any rate there should be some consideration for a man who has lost a limb in the war. As soon as he is adept with his left I am sure he will consider Typesetting, Accounting, Etc. & Etc. Olympia is I am sure a steady rock to you all.

Olympia's husband, Mason, had been killed at Adairsville, during Johnston's retreat toward Atlanta. The man was too big to be a human being and too small to be a locomotive. He had been shot out of the tower of the Bardsley mansion and when he fell three stories and struck the ground he probably made a hole big enough to bury a hog in. The Captain's younger daughter, Olympia, was in reality a woman who affected helplessness and refinement and had never been able to pull a turnip from the garden without weeping over the poor, dear thing. She fluttered and gasped and incessantly tried to demonstrate how sensitive

she was. Mason was a perfect foil and then the Yankees went
and killed him.

Olympia was now living with Elizabeth and Emory in the
remains of their farm in New Hope Church, Georgia, and was
quite likely a heavy weight. He put one hand to his forehead.
My youngest daughter is in reality a bore.

There was a pounding on the wall: Kep-dun! Kep-dun!

He got up and pounded back. Cho-henna! he said. Go to
sleep!

The Captain heard a soothing voice on the other side of the
wall. The way one spoke to restless horses: firm, low-voiced.
Commands that were somehow gentle. Earlier he had heard
Mrs. Gannet and the girl going down the hall to the bathroom.
A small shriek of fear as the toilet flushed. You could hear everything in this hotel. He wished he had spent more money and
had taken rooms in one of the big stone hotels where one's privacy was assured.

> *. . . your husbands having been both of old Georgia State
> regiments would be true to their comrades and so it was
> fate and the Will of the Almighty had led you all to go back
> to Georgia to fight in the War and thus into the heart of the
> Burning but considering what has occurred to other families
> we return thanks for our dear ones who are still with us. I
> know travel is extremely difficult at present but once you are
> here things will be better.*

He paused, went back, and blotted it out from "and thus"
to "Burning" with a corner of torn paper, then struck through

it, held the paper slantwise to the light, and saw that it was un-
readable. Good. No dreadful memories or things that would
induce weeping.

*The recent houses of Senate and Representatives of the State
of Texas have passed a law forbidding the population to carry
sidearms, that is handguns, but at present . . .*

He started to write about the Comanche and Kiowa raids
across the Red River, but saw that once again his news was
falling into the alarming, the frightening, and he wanted his
daughters and Emory and the children to come back to Texas.
They had lived through enough. Their journey to Texas would
be difficult as most bridges in the South had been blown up
or burned during the war and the railroads and rolling stock
shelled to pieces. There was no public money to rebuild. It was
not only Sherman. It had been General Forrest who had blown
up most of the railroads between Tennessee and Mississippi to
keep the Yankees from using them. At any rate, they were all in
tatters. Food and clothing were still scarce. They would have to
apply for passes from the Union Army to travel the rutted and
cratered roads, probably in two wagons with only one man for
two women and two children and that man with only one arm.
They would have to cross the Mississippi at Vicksburg if there
was a ferry. They would have to carry money to buy food and
forage while the roads were crawling with highwaymen.

*. . . but at present we do well without sidearms and there is
no legal constriction against smoothbores and so from time*

to time I enjoy a supper of Quail and Duck. The trumpeters and the whooping cranes are coming back and settle on the Red in their passage. Now my dearest ones enough Gossip, I must come to the important part of my Relations to you which is that I consider you would all do well here in Texas rather than in the Ruined and Devastated States in the East and please consider the land owing to your late Mother. If you all were to return I would be happy once again in the company of my daughters and son-in-law and my grandsons, and since Elizabeth has always been enamored of the process of Law she could begin the legal Discovery and then turn it over to a lawyer adept at fixed-asset litigation.

Yes I know the Spanish land has long been a Chimera in our family but indeed it is there and requires much research. If you would begin the process by writing to Sr. Amistad De Lara, Land Commissioner and archivist of the Spanish Colonial Historical Records, Bexar County Courthouse, and be sure you spell your mother's maiden name correctly, Srta. Maria Luisa Betancort y Real, and the inherited land is una liga y un labor, which means, and I hope you remember your Spanish, both grazing land and garden land, which was legally separated from the Mission Concepcion, that is, Nuestra Señora de la Purísima Concepcion de Acuña (spell it correctly and remember the accents) for Sr. De Lara is a stickler. We have the casa de dueña in San Antonio still as it has been continuously occupied by Betancort descendants who are there now, aged as mummies and complaining because they cannot get white bread and must subsist on tortillas.

Your mother's grandfather, Henri Hipolito Betancort

y Goraz, bought the liga *and the* labor *from the mission but the laws of the Spanish Crown said that all titles had to be registered in Mexico City, a journey of two months at least so it was never registered there and so there are problems with clear title. Not to speak of the fact that after 1821 the Land Registration offices in Mexico City then fell under the Republic of Mexico, notoriously corrupt and I have heard extremely careless with their filing systems. So a shaky title to these lands here came under the Republic of Texas and then the United States and then the Confederacy and now the United States again. There are stacks of moldering papers in Sr. De Lara's offices. You will love it, Elizabeth. You were born to be an ink-stained wretch, my dear.*

I believe the labor *is on the San Antonio River 5 mi. south of Concepcion and the* liga *is on the Balcones Heights amounting all told to more or less three hundred English acres. The Valenzuela family were running sheep and goats on it but last I heard they had deserted the area.*

Kep-dun!

He heard a low sobbing. He bent his head to the paper. He thought Indians never cried. It pulled him away from these legal land questions. It tore his heart.

He closed his eyes and laid down his pen and tried to calm himself. So much had fallen to the old since seven hundred thousand young Southern men were casualties of war. Out of a population of a few million. He must arrange for his family to be together again, he must enter into litigation, he must make a living with his readings, he must deliver this child to her relatives who would no doubt be utterly appalled by what she had become. For a moment he was completely at a loss as to why he had agreed to take her to Castroville.

For Britt. A freed black man. That's why.

In the next room, something broke. More quiet tones from Mrs. Gannet, the unflappable.

No use trying to write anymore.

Your affectionate father, Jefferson Kyle Kidd.

He heard the loud objections in Kiowa as the girl was dragged down the hall to the bathing facilities. One cannot think with a ten-year-old Kiowa-German captive throwing soap and ceramics. After a while they came back and there was more sobbing. Then Mrs. Gannet began to sing.

He bent his head and listened. She had a good voice, a clear light soprano. She sang "Jesus Keep Me Near the Cross" and then "It Is Well with My Soul." He slowly shifted the letter paper and began to fold it. *When peace like a river attendeth my way* . . . very good. At age seventy-one he deserved peace like a river but apparently he wasn't going to get it at present. The town of Dallas beyond the window raised up its new raw-lumber buildings and the air was woven with crashing wheel noises and shouts of the men at the ferry landing. What must the girl think of these man-made bluffs and rigidly straight byways? The sobbing died down. Mrs. Gannet sang "Black Is the Color." Not an easy song to sing unaccompanied. An old folk song in the Dorian mode. The girl was listening. It was much closer to the Indian way of singing. The unexpected turns and strange Celtic intervals. He wondered why he had not in the past year offered his attentions to Mrs. Gannet and then he knew why. Because his daughters felt he should remain forever loyal to the memory of their mother and if they found out about it Olympia and Elizabeth would have had a galvanized tin hissy, one apiece.

At last it was quiet on the other side of the deal board wall. He turned down the kerosene lamp. Nearly eight. Showtime.

TEN

————◦•◦————

A LOW TRAVELING TIDE of gleaming white clouds told of more rain to come. There was good seating at the Broadway. That meant people were more comfortable and would therefore be patient and listen longer. The Captain brought his own bull's-eye lantern as always. He set it on a plant stand to his left, opposite to that of right-handed readers, and trained the light on the dense gray print. He laid down his small gold hunting watch at the top of the podium. At the front double doors two U.S. Army men were stationed, as there were whenever there was a public meeting at any time. Texas was still under military rule.

This might end in a few months if Washington would seat the Texas delegation. The recent election for Texas governor had not been between the old Southern Democrats and the Union-loyal Republicans. No indeed. The old Southern Democratic party was finished in Texas. The fighting was between two factions within the Republicans. The one led by Davis was extreme in its demand for dictatorial powers. The one led by Hamilton, not so much. Both were robbing the state blind.

There was no point in appealing to one's congressman to help clear up land titles in the state. They were too busy lining their pockets. Clearing the Betancort land title would take up Elizabeth's time for years. She would enjoy it very much.

There was a good crowd and he heard the coins ringing into his paint can at the entrance. He greeted the crowd as always, with a statement of thanks to the proprietor of the Broadway, a comment on the state of the roads from Wichita Falls to Spanish Fort and then here. Then he shook out the *London Times*. It was in this way he asked people to enter another realm of the mind. Places far away and mysterious, brought to them by details which they did not understand but which entranced them.

He read of the attempt by the British Colonial government to enumerate the peoples under their rule, a census, in short, and the rebellion of the Hindu tribes against the census takers because married women were not permitted to say aloud the names of their husbands. (Nods; *they are all beyond rational thought in those far countries.*) He read about a great windstorm in London that toppled chimney pots (*What is a chimney pot?* He could see it on their faces.) and then of the new packing plants in Chicago which would take any amount of cattle if they could only get them. In the crowd were men who were contemplating driving cattle all the way to Missouri if they could evade the savage tribes and they listened with deep interest. The Captain read of the Irish pouring into New York City, ragged crowds unloaded from the passenger steamer *Aurora*, of the railroad driving into the plains of the new state of Nebraska, of another eruption of Popocatépetl near Mexico City. Anything but Texas politics.

Someone called, Why are you not reading from Governor Davis's state journal?

The Captain folded his newspapers. He said, Sir, you know very well why. He leaned forward over the podium. His white hair shone, his gold-rim glasses winked in the bull's-eye lantern beam. He was the image of elderly wisdom and reason. Because there would be a fistfight here within moments, if not shooting. Men have lost the ability to discuss any political event in Texas in a reasonable manner. There is no debate, only force. In point of fact, regard the soldiers beyond the door.

He slapped his newspapers into the portfolio. He said, I am an aggregator of news from distant places, and as for the Austin paper and the *Herald,* you can read them for yourselves. The Captain shut the flap on his portfolio and buckled it tight. And fight among yourselves on your own time and not during my reading.

He heard *hear, hear!* from among the wet and shining heads of the men who held their hats in their hands and from some of the women in their pancake hats and their bonnets.

He blew out the bull's-eye lantern and took it and the portfolio and stepped down from the stage. Among the crowd filtering out he saw, with a dropping feeling, the pale-haired man and the two Caddos he had last seen in Wichita Falls and perhaps Spanish Fort. He knew the Indians were Caddos because of their blunt-cut hair, sliced off just at the jawline, their shirts of a dark blue with a tiny print of yellow flowers. The Caddos liked printed calico. The blond man sat relaxed in a theater chair with an ankle cocked up on the other leg and his hat on the point of his knee. He was watching the Captain.

As the Captain stepped down from the lectern people came to their feet; some followed him. He shook the hands that were held out to him and accepted thanks and compliments. Everybody smelled like wet wool and camphor and a sneezing small woman said, Thank you, Captain, and shaking her hand gave him a moment's pleasure, to see her bright cheeks. Perhaps he had taken her away from worry and preoccupation for a short while, what the Captain called the "hard thoughts." And a man with a grave look and a silver lapel badge in the shape of a shamrock from Hancock's Second Artillery Corps, Union. The Captain shook his hand firmly. No matter what side you were on, if you had survived Gettysburg you were to be congratulated. Perhaps he had briefly escorted the man's mind into the lands of the imagination—far places, crisp ice mountains, falling chimney pots, tropical volcanoes.

The manager of the Broadway came to him with the Captain's share of the money. He had made nearly twenty dollars in good U.S. silver. He wadded the sack of coins into his coat pocket. A man went around putting out the candles in the chandeliers with a long-handled snuffer. Inside the Broadway Playhouse it grew darker and darker.

Captain, said the blond man. He stood up. My name is Almay.

And these are your friends, said Captain Kidd.

They are. The blond man put on his hat.

You followed me from Wichita Falls. I think I saw you at Spanish Fort.

I have business here and there, said Almay. How much do you want for the girl?

Captain Kidd stopped stone cold. For a moment, a long moment, he stood expressionless and utterly still. *I was wrong. Somebody does want her.* He put on his own hat. He settled it carefully on his white hair. He looked down at Almay, several inches shorter. He blinked once, slowly, as he buttoned up his black overcoat. He noted the two Caddos directly behind him.

Almay said, You know the Army don't patrol the roads here like they do up on the Red. I could catch you on the road and just take her, you know. But I am being a fair and straightforward man with you. How much?

The Captain said, I hadn't settled on a price.

Or found a buyer.

No. Nor found a buyer.

Well, let's consider it. I'm not close-fisted. I pay for what I want.

Do you, now?

Captain Kidd had left the .38 back in the hotel room. It was too big to pack around under the three-button frock coat he wore for readings and it was heavy. Perhaps it was best. The feeling that was at present almost overwhelming him would have led him to draw and shoot the man on the spot. And then where would Johanna be when he was in jail?

Yes. Tell me the name of anybody who says otherwise.

I couldn't be bothered, said Captain Kidd. Of course, I want assurances that the girl will be well treated.

A bit better than what the Indians did to them, said Almay. His lips flattened out into a strange, stiff smile. At least she'll get paid for it. Blond girls are premium, premium.

Do tell. The Captain nodded amiably. His mind was tearing

ahead like a steam engine into the next hour, the next day. How much ammunition he had, if they knew where he was going, and if they did, if they knew what road he would take.

He said, I tell you what, Almay. Meet me tomorrow morning at the Tyler Stage Roadhouse at about seven. We'll work out a price. I did not take in much tonight and I am in need of funds.

Good. Almay's eyelids seemed heavy. He had gray eyes and the thick and colorless skin of people from Scandinavia or Russia. He seemed half asleep or he was dreaming of some other world that was not this world, a place fragmented and without illumination.

THE CAPTAIN TOUCHED his hat to the U.S. Army sergeant in blue at the door, something not many men would have done, and hurried out. The air was damp; condensation sparkled on every surface and lay in a billion dots on the roof shingles. He saw Almay and the Caddos turn north up Trinity and in the opposite direction from his little hotel on Stemmons Ferry Road.

He walked fast through the unpaved streets to Gannet's Livery and called out to the oafish stableman, harnessed the roan mare and then backed her into the shafts, settled the collar, hooked up the trace chains, turned the wagon facing out. He changed clothes as fast as he had ever changed in his life. Into the wagon he threw his portfolio and the bag of coins, and wrapped up the remains of their supper in the frying pan. He put his formal black reading clothes and coat over his arm. He stroked Pasha's neck, wiped the flyspecks out of his eyes, and then tied him on behind. He left the tin pail for the man to return to the cookshop.

He said, I am going to get Mrs. Gannet. We will settle up in half an hour.

Hour, said the stableman. He sat up in his blankets where he had been sleeping in an empty stall with his handkerchief, for some reason, tied around his head and an empty bottle clinked on the nailheads in the floor. Half. Damned hurry. People running around middle of night. Then he fell back in the straw.

The Captain trotted down the dark streets of Dallas and then turned on Stemmons Ferry to the hotel. A few dim-lit windows here and there and they seemed sinister and spying. He ran upstairs and went to his room and packed the carpetbag. He hefted it and went next door. He rapped hard and fast.

Mrs. Gannet opened it in a nightgown that must have had eleven yards in the hem, her dark brown hair undone. He could smell the sulphur of a match; she had quickly lit their lamp. She wore a forest-green wrapper over the nightgown and her hair hung down her back and shoulders in shining planes. Her mouth was open. Behind her Johanna sat up out of her bed, fully awake, and planted both her square feet on the floor.

Mrs. Gannet was both calm and alert. Captain? she said.

Quick, he said. We have to leave tonight.

BEFORE HE STEPPED up on the foot plate he removed his hat to Mrs. Gannet and expressed his thanks. She was outraged and shocked at what Almay had said. She did not know Almay but she would know him now. Her eyes sparked in the light of the lantern she carried in one hand. She was furious. It gave her a bright and animated look and he was felled on the instant. He took her hand; it was short and strong and on her wrist was a bangle of silver and some sparkling red gems.

I hope I may do myself the honor of calling on you on my return? said the Captain. He smiled. I was thinking of picnics on the banks of the Trinity.

First, return, she said. And take care, my dear man.

He hesitated and then bent and kissed her lightly on the cheek.

When they pulled out into the nighttime streets she stood holding the lantern, and in its light motes of hay sifted around her like fireflies.

THEY SET OUT down the Waxahachie Road to the south because Almay and his friends would expect them to take the Meridian Road southwest. Then later in the night they could cut west and get back on the Meridian Road. He hoped that when Almay and Company saw no fresh tracks or sight of them on the Meridian Road they would turn back and look for them elsewhere. Maybe he and Johanna could gain three or four hours on them.

They trotted into the chain of hills that lay southeast of Dallas. They were called the Brownwood Hills. Before daylight they should come to a country cut up by the Brazos River into ravines and sliding red-rock cliffs, covered by live oak which had never been logged out. Some of them were as big around as millstones. He wanted to reach the river by daylight and pull off the road, up high, and watch for their pursuers. It would not take them long to bribe the stable hand for information. The man was a drinker. Drinkers were easy.

The rain had cleared and so they went at a good round trot. The sky was washed with clouds in one rainy line after another and the moon at three-quarters full seemed to be rolling backward. The road before them was indistinct and without perspective. It was difficult to estimate distances in moonlight. The Captain intended to put as many miles as possible between them and Almay and the Caddos before daylight.

The Captain was not averse to a fight but he was poorly armed. He took out the revolver and stuck it in his waistband on the right side, butt forward. He needed a holster. The shotgun was a twelve-gauge bolt action, a single shot at a time, and all he had was bird shot. He had only one box of cartridges for the revolver. He thought there might be close to twenty rounds. There had been no money to buy another box or a holster when first they came into Dallas and now late at night the town was shuttered and closed and those who were about were not people he wanted to meet.

The shotgun lay at the Captain's feet under the dashboard, longways, loaded, the little lever on safety and he worried about it. The lever was too easy to shift. It was loose. He could grab for it and fire off a shot right into one of the horses before he could bring it to bear if he were not careful.

It was March 5 and cold, his breath fumed and his old muffler was dank with the steam. Above and behind them the Dipper turned on its great handle as if to pour night itself out onto the dreaming continent and each of its seven stars gleamed from between the fitful passing clouds. After several hours he found a track going west and took it and within two hours they were on the Meridian Road. The country here was sparsely settled and only occasionally policed. Indian raids out of the north were a given. They pressed on.

The girl sat in the wagon bed behind wrapped in the thick red and black *jorongo*. There was no method by which he could explain anything to her but she did not need explanations. Her family and her tribe had fought with the Utes, their ancient enemies, and the Caddos. They had conducted a long guerrilla warfare with Texas settlers and Texas Rangers and then with the U.S. Army. Often enough they had faced the howling, striving demons of the open plains: hunger, tornadoes, scarlet fever. She didn't need to be told anything except that there were enemies in pursuit and she had already figured that out.

The road was open before them, a two-track stretch in the pale of the moon, rolling over the lifts and falls of the prairie country of central Texas. They passed a farmhouse set back among trees. The farm buildings appeared to be great dozing animals that had gathered near the house in the night. There was a light shining in a window. Somebody was waiting up for somebody. Pasha tested the air for the scent of a mare. Had there been one he would have called out, making promises he would never be able to fulfill, but since all he could smell was a donkey and another gelding he held his peace and trotted on. Here and there were copses of post oak holding up wiry armatures of limb and twig, rattling with old brown leaves, and in the cold night air a hissing swift shape passed in front of them.

The girl cried out. *Sau-Podle!* She bent herself forward and carried the red wool up around her nose as if she would not breathe the air. Sau-Podle brought news of a death; soon, here. It cut the air like a blade and trailed plump legs like a child's in fluffy pantaloons.

Great horned, said the Captain. Ignore it, Johanna. Pretend it was a night hawk.

ELEVEN

———————

A T FIRST LIGHT the Captain and Johanna were only a mile or so from the Brazos. As they went on they came to the little road that ran alongside the north bank. Then they came to a place he remembered as Carlyle Springs. The spring fed down out of a bluff of red sandstone into a ravine and then into the Brazos itself. It sparkled all the way down, jumping in transparent streams from pool to pool. The Captain looked up and thought he saw a way to get up there; a faint wagon track zigzagging up the slope.

He turned Fancy off the road and went uphill. After a hundred yards he had to get down and lead the mare through agarita and spiky young live oaks that tore at the underside but all he could think of was *Get under cover, get under cover.* He felt like he was pulling the load of the world behind him, Fancy and the girl jolting around in the driver's seat and Pasha scrambling behind. Everything was dripping wet and bedewed and soon he was soaked to the knees.

At the top he found the only flat place to stop. There were

trees and thickets of sumac to give them some concealment. Some stumps; somebody had been up here cutting fence posts. From a layered stack of red sandstone, crenellated and thick as a barbican, he could see the road below.

He bent over with his hands on his knees to relieve his back muscles. He was stiff from the long night's drive. Everything hurt. He straightened up and turned to her with the wrapped bacon in his hand. She took it from him, dropped the tailgate, and laid it down.

I cook! She smiled up at him. Then she held out a piece of divinity candy. Good horse lady, she said. Eat, Kep-dun. Her little face was round as an apple.

He returned the smile. Yes, very good, he said. He ate the piece of divinity and the sugar hit his bloodstream in a rush. He took off his hat and ran his fingers through his white hair. His coat hung open to the morning wind. He felt in his pockets for his pipe.

The girl collected dry wood in her skirt as if happy to discover that skirts were good for something after all. He handed her the match safe and she started the fire in the little cookstove. With the butcher knife she expertly carved the bacon. She sang to herself. This was life as she knew it, and it was good. No roofs, no streets. Her new-washed taffy hair flew in loose ribbons in the morning breeze. Every so often she lifted her head to run her gaze over the live oaks around them and listen for an enemy presence. Then she went back to slinging rashers into the skillet.

The Captain stuffed tobacco into his kaolin pipe. And here he was in his mild and mindless way still roaming, still reading out the news of the world in the hope that it would do some good, but in the end he must carry a weapon in his belt and he had a child to protect and no printed story or tale would alter that. He considered the men who must be following them and also that the smell of tobacco smoke carried far and wide, far more than meat smoke, so on second thought he laid down the pipe.

He unharnessed Fancy and tied her beside Pasha and rubbed them both down with a rice-straw brush. If the Captain and Johanna had to run for it they would do better on horseback than in the wagon. He paused over the saddle and blankets. Not yet. But he found Pasha's riding bridle in the heap of tack and laid it over a wheel where it would be ready to hand.

He pulled on his riding boots with the undershot heels and then his spurs and shoved in the toggles to fix them and keep them from ringing. From his pockets he took out his gold watch and some pennies and his penknife and laid them on the tailgate. He wanted nothing about him that would clink, make a noise. He took out the revolver and once again made sure every chamber was full. He put it back into his waistband. The eight-inch barrel made it feel like he was carrying an axe handle. Whitewing doves sat up in the oaks and shifted from one pink foot to another and bobbed and sang because they wanted to come to water at the spring but were afraid.

The Captain wished he could go back down to the road to see how much of the wagon was visible from there. He guessed probably the top boards. He did not know how soon Almay and his friends might have started from Dallas after them. Probably at about seven-thirty, eight in the morning when he did not show up at the Tyler Stage Roadhouse. When they saw no tracks on the Meridian Road, he hoped they would have doubled back to the Waxahachie Road and stayed on it. With luck they would be far away to the east bumbling along and crying out, Where did they go? Where did they go? But they would wise up soon enough and they were on horseback and therefore faster.

He did not go down. They might catch him down there on foot with a long climb back up to the wagon among the rocks. He lay on his stomach and watched the road. It was red dirt, two tracks with a strip of mullein and Indian grass in the middle. He could see two sections through the trees, one about a half-mile away and another piece just below.

He wiped at his tired eyes and then took up his guard duty again. In the increasing light of day the Captain thought he saw the moving and reflective slash of a horse's tail. The doves became silent. Hm, he said. He climbed up to the wagon seat for a better view.

It was perhaps fifty degrees. A thin watery sun laid its gunmetal shine on the country below. The hills were ridges widely separated from one another in great tree-covered waves, as if they were drifting apart from one another across the stone underpinnings of the earth. On the horizon of cedar-covered hills, a thick billowing of smoke rose into the sky. Somebody was burning slash or stubble about three or four miles away.

The little stove erupted in a singing clatter of broken pipe and scattered coals. The hurtling skillet lid sailed away over a wave of flying hot grease. Another earsplitting *Bang!* Bacon and coffee spun into the air.

The girl was under the wagon in less than a second. The

Captain fell sideways off the seat. He landed on his left side. It was quicker and safer than standing up to climb down. He scrambled under the wagon. Another round hit the sideboards above him and splinters sprayed into the air. He thought of the flour keg with the .38 ammunition in it.

They won't want to kill the horses and they won't want to take a chance on killing the girl. He lifted himself on his elbows and made a reassuring gesture. She was flat on her stomach and her face was turned sideways to him, keeping her eyes on his square old hawk's face. They were lying among rocks and small spiny agarita; a lizard fled in a running of dark chevrons. *They're firing up from the ravine. They have rifles.*

The Captain crawled from under the wagon to the edge of the caprock and found a notch in it. He pulled out the revolver. Another shot from the right, different place. They had both been from the right. So where was the third man? He spat on his hand and then smeared it on his revolver barrel and then sifted dust over it. The Smith and Wesson with its long barrel was accurate but nowhere near as accurate as a rifle. And it didn't have the range. Their rifles were good for two hundred yards or more. They could stay out of range and blast away at him till the cows came home.

The shotgun was good only for close work; he had only fifteen shells of light Number Seven, what they called turkey shot or dove shot, which would at most pepper somebody's face with a permanent tattoo unless you jammed it right up against them at face-to-face range and that was a situation he would not be likely to survive. In the shot box were powder and caps and hulls to make up more shotgun shells, as if it mattered. He lay still and felt running tremors in his belly. Fear for himself, for the girl. *Help me.*

He turned and saw Johanna crawling toward him, dragging the box of .38 ammunition. She had got it out of the flour keg. It was covered with flour, so were her hands.

He took the box and then pointed sternly to the wagon. She wriggled back.

This was not the first time that someone had wanted to kill him but the other times had been what one might call fair fights. The two rifle shots sounded to the Captain as if they had come from Henrys. A Spencer made a flatter, barking sound. But it could have been the gunpowder they were using. He smelled the gunpowder smoke rising up from below in long windless strands that snarled in the cedar. His mouth was dry. They had been traveling the entire night and he was weary and the cloudy light was diffuse so it was difficult to see.

He had not thought they would turn so quickly to murder. He had thought if they caught up, they would bluster, threaten, offer a certain amount in silver, perhaps even claim they were the girl's relatives. He saw himself pointing the long barrel of the Smith and Wesson into their faces and saying something like, Begone or I will blow you through. This was clearly not going to happen. Human aggression and depravity still managed to astonish him. He had been caught by surprise.

The girl was under the wagon. She was listening. Then she lifted her hands and whipped her long hair into a braid and tied it off with a piece of lace edging she tore from her skirt. She was not astonished. Not at all.

He lay still in the crumbled stone and blue-green agarita behind the protection of the caprock. He waited. He and Johanna were exposed to the wooded slope behind them, higher ground, but it was a good quarter mile away. Almay and the Caddos were coming up from below. The wagon must have been just barely exposed. He waited. The wind was cold.

He heard, remotely, the lever action of another Henry and then saw another puff of gunpowder smoke below, from behind a long slanting buttress of red stone on the right side of the ravine. Instantly afterward he heard a sharp, flat crack and the noise of the wagon being hit again. Splinters burst into the air and rained around him. Pasha fell back on his halter rope but it did not break so he came up straight again. He wasn't hit. Fancy was more determined and tore her halter rope loose and went crashing away into the trees and stopped. She was hung up on something.

The Captain waited for the other, or two others if they were all armed with rifles. He had to hoard his revolver ammunition and watch for the best shot even if they were right in his face. It seemed his eyes would start from his head. He had to shut them for a moment. Then a .45 long Colt round struck to his right like a hammerhead, about six feet away and then he heard the muzzle blast. He didn't turn his head but only noted where the smoke came from. It had also come from the right side of the ravine, farther down. Number three. The shot did not have that deep, biting bark of a rifle, so it was a revolver. They had all three come up single file on one side. Stupid. They were overconfident. They were up against nothing but an old man and a girl.

In some ways he wouldn't mind going out in a blaze of glory. Seventy-one was a good long time to have lived. But then there was Johanna.

The mild, watery sun of early March poured down a shadowless light. Not many reflections. Another shot. It chipped the face of the dark, dense limestone to his left. He did not duck nor glance in that direction but watched for the smoke.

He saw it. Same rifle. Two, that's all they had. The third man was the odd man out and had to make do with a revolver like himself.

Then he saw a man jump from one buttress of rusty-red stone to another to cross the ravine to the other side. He was carrying a rifle. The Captain fired three times, chipping the stone around the man, sending up sprays of cedar duff and the sumac leaves like little airborne ears. It was one of the Caddos. They were trying to nail him between two lines of fire; a rifle to his left and a rifle and a handgun to his right.

A brief glimpse; the Caddo was wearing a heavy leather glove on his left hand. So he was right, they did have Henrys. There was no floor arm on the Henry and its hot barrel and the magazine tube had to be handled with a glove. Another shot. He waited for the flash of a rifle barrel on his left, within the range of his revolver, saw it, fired twice and heard a yell and the rifle flew away and got wedged among the rocks.

Got him. At least he had knocked the rifle out of his hand. And now the stupid fool was going to go after it.

He aimed and waited. He was sure the Caddo was going to try to retrieve his precious expensive rifle. *Go for it, man.* Over on the other side of the ravine he caught a glimpse of the crown of a hat. He was too smart for that. It was on a stick.

Johanna, get back!

The girl ignored him. She was edging along the caprock to his right. She ducked in and out between the great tabular sections of red sandstone, holding on to the unforgiving rock with her bare hands. She peered over, she ducked back. She carried the stove lid lifter in one hand and now she began to lever at the base of a flat layer of stone. She had pulled the back hem of her skirts between her legs and tucked it into the dainty belt at her waist in front so it looked as if she were wearing big Turkish pantaloons. She was still barefoot. She looked like the engravings he had seen of Circassian children in their rags and bandoliers fighting the Russian troops somewhere in the Pontus. This was clearly not her first gunfight. *Mao sap-he,* she said. *Caddos. The Ring-in-the-nose people. They will die.* She didn't care if he did not understand her, it was simply important to say, *They will die.*

The Captain turned back to his notch and through the leaves on the left he saw the Caddo's black hair glinting as he dodged from rock to rock, down the ravine, going for his rifle. He fired again. A yell, then whimpering. One wounded. How bad he didn't know. Sweat ran from under his hat, from the tattered sweatband and into his eyes and he wiped his eyes on his shoulder one after the other, quickly. He was surprised when he saw he had to reload. He had not thought he had fired so many rounds. His hands had flour on them from the box of shells.

Johanna was still levering at the base of a slab of stone with the lifter. To his amazement she tipped it up, and then over, and it rolled end over end like a flat plate on edge, leaping downhill, smashed in half on an outthrust boulder and then shattered and fell in pieces upon somebody. There was a deep shout, almost a grunt, and a man fell forward out of concealment and rolled.

Good girl, he said. Demon child! He laughed as he fired again and again, careless of the expenditure of ammunition. Then he was furious with himself; the man was in his sights and yet he could not hit him. Then the man disappeared.

TWELVE

H E HAD TWENTY cartridges left. He clicked out the cylinder and reloaded.

He smiled at her as she came back. You are most amazing, he said.

She acknowledged this with a grave nod and turned her attention back to their enemies.

Another rifle round shattered stone in front of him like an explosion. He bent his head against flying chips and felt a strange electrical pain all over his skull, a nerve pain, then he couldn't see out of his right eye. He wiped at it quickly and it cleared and he watched for the smoke. He saw it down to the right, again. She had probably hit the man with the handgun. The stream of water chattered busily down the ravine and here and there shone like glass. The Captain wiped again at his eye and then looked at his hand. It was wet with blood. A blade of stone blown off the rock had struck him over the right eye but he thought it would stop bleeding in a minute or so. He must not be incapacitated, he must not be killed because he knew very well what they would do with the girl. Some people were born unsupplied with a human conscience and those people needed killing.

He tried to think how many of them were wounded. He might have shot the Henry rifle barrel out of alignment. He thought he had hit the man on the left but how badly he didn't know. Johanna had wounded another by tipping a rock down on him.

He bent his head to his knuckles. His shirt was spotty with blood. He considered his choices. They could run for it, riding double on Pasha. Get Fancy loose and she would follow them. If they gained enough distance from Almay and the Caddos he could stop long enough to put her on the mare, but Fancy was a dear slow creature with her out-of-alignment front leg and prone to stumble. They could try to reach that distant smoke on the horizon.

Johanna crept forward and brought the leather water bottle to him. The Captain rolled onto his back and poured it down. Some ran down the sides of his mouth. He capped it. Almay and his evil minions had the spring water trickling down the ravine but he and Johanna had only this one canteen. He handed it back to her.

Useless thoughts again and again of why he had not carried more ammunition, why he had not bought more. Because they left Dallas in the middle of the night, that's why.

Then the girl held out a wet cloth to him and he took it and wiped his forehead and eye. Lucky it was his right eye because it was his left eye that he aimed with. It was a shallow cut but the blade of stone seemed to have hit a nerve because it made a crawling sharp pain all over his scalp. It didn't matter. He could see out of both eyes now. His vision was very good. The animals down below probably thought he was half blind with old age. Well surprise surprise. He turned over on his stomach. After this little silence they would be eaten up with curiosity. He caught a glimpse of a rifle barrel within range of the revolver. He laid the long eight-inch barrel in a notch; he fired carefully and listened happily to another shout of pain.

Kep-dun, she said.

He looked into her worried dark blue eyes. My dear, he said. Let's face facts.

He flipped open the cylinder of the revolver and turned his hand so that she could see it was empty. In his other hand he held the remaining fourteen rounds.

She reached out for the shotgun and looked at him.

No good, he said. No. He showed her one of the shells. Nothing but light Number Seven bird shot. It would not even carry very far. He pointed toward Pasha. Then he pointed to her. His bay saddle horse stood stiff as a china figure with fright and his ears were rigidly fixed at full cock toward the ravine. The horse might prove difficult, but among the Plains Indians, even young children could ride and ride well.

Go, he said. He made an "away" motion with his hand. Go.

He had made up his mind and his expression was firm and unsmiling.

They were calling up to him. They were trying to make a deal. *Haina, haina.* No, she would not go.

Get on the horse and go, he said. He slid backward and got hold of Pasha's riding bridle from off the front wheel rim and held it out to her. The Captain knew that with two of the men below wounded she might have a chance. Damn it, go.

Haina.

Suddenly he felt very tired. He could not deal with her and their attackers all at once. With his last fourteen rounds clattering in his hand he crawled again tight behind the lip of rock and found his notch. He loaded the cylinder and wasted three more shots trying to ricochet a round into Almay, who was behind the buttress on the right-hand side. Then one of the Caddos appeared, darting up the ravine and into cover again, and that caused him to uselessly expend another two shots. It was his judgment that was failing him as much as his strength. The only good thing was that the Caddo had a bloody hand.

Johanna, get on that horse and go.

For a moment he dropped his head on his forearm. When he lifted it there was a kind of bloody eye-socket print on it. She had gone somewhere. He pressed the wet cloth against his eyebrow. Again the strange flashes of nerve pain all over his skull. Then he saw her crawling toward him with the shotgun in one hand and the shot box in the other. Somehow she had managed to stack the bag of coins on top of the shot box and shove that along too. She was covered in dirt. He supposed he was too. She pressed the bag of coins toward him and gestured down the ravine.

Johanna, they are not going to be bought off, he said. He patted her arm. Her hair was coming out of the braid and it hung over her young, childish face in swags. He said, They can't be bribed, they are not going to be made to go away with offers of coin. He looked into her anxious blue eyes and a terrible thought came to him. He felt his eyes leaking tears or sweat.

She could not be allowed to fall into their hands. Never. Never. He had eight shots left, six in the cylinder and two in hand. He said, It won't work my dear.

She pushed the shotgun toward him.

He shook his head. Useless. He opened a shell and poured the tiny lead beads out into his hand and showed her.

Another shot from the left. It struck near one of the shafts of the wagon. The Caddo had got his rifle again and was shooting, wounded or not, and the smoke told him the man had gained higher ground. More than fifty yards away. If he got above them and started shooting down on them they were in serious, serious trouble. The Captain watched for him, saw the bright shifting of black hair.

He felt Johanna tugging at his sleeve. He looked down.

She held up one of the shotgun shells.

It was loaded with dimes.

He stared at the shell resting on Johanna's outstretched palm.

Then the Captain reached out for it even as another round smashed into the front of the stone in front of him. He jumped but didn't duck. He lay back and hefted the shell. The dimes fit perfectly into the paper tube of a twelve-gauge hull.

Well, I'll be damned.

It was very heavy. He looked at the cap. She charged it with the powder charger. He saw her work the thumb lever that gave out twenty grains at a time: one, two, three, four, eighty grains of powder. A heavy load for his old shotgun. The Captain tossed the shell full of dimes up and down in his hand and smiled.

This is amazing, he said. He laughed. Ten years old and a wizard of field expedience.

With the weight of the dimes and the powder charge the shotgun had just become something like a small cannon. Not only that but heavy things flew far and fast and so it might give him a range of close to two hundred yards.

He couldn't stop laughing. By God, by God, he said. They had a chance to get out of this. Everything had changed now. Good girl, Johanna, good girl. My dear little warrior.

He did not notice that he stank of cordite and that Johanna's hands were white with flour and that both of them were coated with the red dirt of the Brazos country. The Captain found that suddenly he was no longer tired. She smiled back at him with her bright child's teeth and then the Captain held up one hand. *Wait.* She nodded.

First they had some ruses and deceptions to accomplish. He took up one of the dove-shot shells and loaded the old shotgun. As he laid the barrel into the notch he saw her loading yet more dimes into shells, ramming in the wads with a stick, pouring out powder from the old spring-loaded charger, ramming another wad and finally twisting each hull firmly shut.

He fired down the ravine and heard the light beads of Number Seven Dove tinkle harmlessly on the stone.

Far below, Almay's laugh rang out. He called, That all you got?

Come closer and you'll find out, you son of a bitch, the Captain called back.

I'm scared. You're shooting cake decorations or something at me, Almay shouted in reply.

Well come on, then, said the Captain.

He wondered where the Caddos were. Nursing their wounds, hopefully, or better yet, busy bleeding to death. He loaded another Number Seven and fired. It sprayed out its tiny beads into the air as if it had sneezed poppy seeds. He glanced at Johanna. She was busy stacking more dimes into hulls.

Listen to me, said Almay. He was still hidden behind one of the stone buttresses.

I don't seem to have a choice, called the Captain.

You should be good at a bargain. This ain't your first rodeo, here.

They don't need to make a deal. He thinks everything is on his side. What he wants is to kill me and take the girl and the horses. They'll burn the wagon. It's too recognizable. Curative Waters. *He wants to get close enough to kill me without hitting the girl. He's not sure of his aim. He's shooting uphill. Always difficult.*

He worked the bolt and the old hull jumped out smoking and she grabbed it. Now he slipped one of her dime shells into the breech. The weight of it should give him a good hundred and seventy, hundred and eighty yards if not more. He laid the barrel into the notch.

What's your deal? he called.

Reasonable! I can be reasonable.

Come up, we'll talk.

The blond man held his hat out from the edge of the buttress. There was a hole in it. Captain, he said. You was trying to hit me in the head, here. That's serious malicious intent. We have some serious talking to do.

So?

Listen to me, said Almay.

You already said that. Stop repeating yourself.

Now, let's make some kind of deal here.

Why was he delaying? The Captain knew the only reason was to keep him talking while the Caddos crept up. Far to his left a small trickle of sand and rocks spilled down the ravine.

Well speak up, then, said the Captain. Stop your goddamn dithering. I hate dithering.

By now Almay knew the range of the shotgun and its dove shot. He walked confidently out from behind his buttress of stone. He also thought the Captain was out of revolver ammunition. Clearly he was not shooting it and had reverted, in his desperation, to the shotgun and its pepper-light loads. Almay advanced up the ravine. Here and there the water of Carlyle Springs had worn the red sandstone layers down to the strata below, hard and marblelike. White and pure and level. They were like irregular steps going down the ravine, carved through the eons. Since Noah, perhaps. Almay carried his hat in one hand and took long steps to reach from one plate to the next in his knee-high boots. His hair was dark with sweat. They had ridden hard to catch up.

I tell you what, Almay called. You put down that shotgun and I'll make sure my men empty their magazines and we can have a conversation.

Two hundred yards, then a little closer. *Come on, come on.*

Certainly. I'm putting it down as we speak.

The Captain aimed very carefully. He was not sure what the coins would do, or the extra-heavy powder charge. So he aimed for the V of Almay's open shirt collar and pulled the trigger.

The dimes roared out of the muzzle at six hundred feet per second with a muzzle blast two feet long. The gunsmoke expanded in a great thick cloud and the stock slammed back into the Captain's shoulder almost hard enough to dislocate it. He struck Almay in the forehead with a load of U.S. mint ten-cent pieces. As the coins flew out of the paper tube they turned on edge so that when they hit Almay's forehead it looked as if his head had been suddenly printed with hyphens. The hyphens all began to spout blood. Almay fell backward, his head downhill. All the Captain could see was his boot soles.

He jerked off his hat and shoved it between the butt of the stock and his shoulder. Then without turning his head he held out his hand and a dime-loaded shotgun shell was slapped into it, he shoved it in, shot the bolt home, brought the sights to bear on the scrambling Caddos. Another great bellow like a cannon and silver coins hissed through the air faster than sight and they sparkled and ricocheted all down the ravine. The roar of the overloaded twelve-gauge sounded like a grenade had gone off. Ten-cent pieces slammed edge-on into a wounded Caddo's backside. A shower of bright flying money tore through the trees lower down and clipped branches and leaves of the live oak, spanged off stone, chipped the skull crown of the Caddo in the rear so that he instinctively turned around to fight and the Captain unloaded on him again. Silver like tearing sequins sliced sideways through their blousy shirtsleeves and turned their hats into colanders.

By God, I believe that was a good two hundred and fifty yards, the Captain said.

Finally he leaned back against his red stone barbican. His nerves were glowing like fuses and he was not tired anymore. *I got them. I did it. We did it.*

She held up another shell, laughing and smiling.

No, my dear. He was sucking air. His eyebrow still hurt. We need the money to buy supplies.

He lay back against the rock breathing slowly. Johanna jumped to her feet, standing straight as a willow wand. She lifted her face to the sun and began to chant in a high, tight voice. Her taffy hair flew in thick strands, powdered with flour, and she took up the butcher knife and held the blade above her head and began to sing. *Hey hey Chal an aun!* Their enemies had run before them. They had fled in terror, they were faint of heart, their hands were without strength, *Hey hey hey! My enemies have been sent to the otherworld, they have been sent to the place that is dark blue, where there is no water, hey hey hey! Coiguu Khoe-duuey!*

We are hard and strong, the Kiowa!

Far below the Caddos heard the Kiowa triumph chant, the scalping chant, and when they struck the bottom of the ravine where it bled out into the Brazos they did not even stop to fill their canteens.

Then she climbed over the lip of rock with her skirts and petticoats wadded into Turkish pantaloons and the butcher knife held high. She was halfway down before the Captain came after her and got hold of her skirt.

She had been on her way to scalp Almay.

No, my dear, we don't . . . it's not done, he said.

Haain-a?

No. Absolutely not. No. No scalping. He lifted her up and swung her up over the ledges of stone and then followed. He said, It is considered very impolite.

THIRTEEN

———◆———

He reharnessed and took up all his small possessions from the tailgate, slammed it shut. He had to find a place to cross the Brazos soon. Going back downhill the Captain rode the brake. The shafts lunged up around Fancy's shoulders on the steep grade and the brake chocks screamed on the axles. All the stuff in the wagon bed ended up in a heap against the back of the driver's seat with Johanna tossed among the tools and food and blankets, holding the revolver. He had unloaded it but she seemed happier with it in her hands. They were frayed and dirty. They both looked like they had been dragged through a knothole. As the wagon plunged downhill among the red rock and stiff brush he prayed they would not break a tie-rod and that the cracked iron tire would hold.

They made it to the bottom and the road in one piece with all possessions and horses still in hand.

The Captain's nerves were humming like telegraph wires in a wind and he knew in a little while he would be close to collapse. He searched every copse of live oaks and when they reached the Brazos, every shadow in the pecan flats. The road ran along the north side of the river, a shy and obsequious road that dodged every bank and lift and wound through the pecan trees and never insisted on its own way. He searched out every road bank ahead of him as they went. He was ready to shoot somebody else if need be. He must slow down. For Johanna, he needed to quiet himself; he must appear calm and assured. The Caddos would bury Almay under a pile of rocks and quietly slip back into Oklahoma. Someday somebody would find the bones and wonder whose they were. Almay would run his child prostitution ring no more, his brains blown out by the coin of the realm, *hey hey hey*. The Captain's heart finally calmed.

That night he dusted his cut forehead with gray wound powder, and then slept like a dead man without his usual war nightmares that should have been brought about by the fight, but somehow they passed him by. Perhaps they sought out someone else. Perhaps he was not on their map this night.

He woke up to a clean and tidy camp under the pecan trees that stood high and airy above them. He heard the noise of a little stream nearby running into the Brazos and the hush, hush sound of small new pecan leaves in the breeze. He heard Johanna crying out, Eat! Now you eat! And the mare's bell ringing as the horses grazed. He took the plate from her and ate carefully. The blue smoke from the little stovepipe lay low and drifted. They were all right, he and the girl were alive. They were having a calm breakfast among the pecan trees, new leaves like green dots with their shadows making slow polkas back and forth over them and the *Curative Waters* golden letters.

He pressed one hand to his right eyebrow. The cut was a little swollen but all right. He could for a brief time work as hard as a younger man but it always took much longer to recover. He must recover. They had far to go.

The horses needed rest and care as much as he did. He would have to teach this to Johanna. The Plains Indians did not expend much care on their horses. They rode them hard and as a last resort ate them. He went down Fancy and Pasha's legs to check for swelling but they were all right. They had last been shod up in Bowie but before long they would need new ones. He straightened up again with some effort; he could almost hear the jointed sound as one vertebrae settled on another.

He sat on his carpetbag and leaned against a wheel. His mind kept going back to the fight and to put it aside he watched Pasha graze and drank black coffee and smoked his pipe. Johanna played in the stream like a six-year-old. She turned over rocks and sang and splashed. To comfort himself and slow down his mind he thought of his time as a courier, a runner, and Maria Luisa and his daughters. Maybe life is just carrying news. Surviving to carry the news. Maybe we have just one message, and it is delivered to us when we are born and we are never sure what it says; it may have nothing to do with us personally but it must be carried by hand through a life, all the way, and at the end handed over, sealed.

He was not really rested but well enough. They went on.

THE NEXT DAY at noon they came to a place called the Brazos ferry. The Brazos unwound slow green coils and smoke from slash fires lay low and drifted at the height of a man's head. There was no ferry. He could see the ferry landing on the other side, downstream about a hundred yards where the current would push them. The landing looked good; it looked like a hard bottom. The river was up so things might have changed. Loads of sand and silt could have been laid over the landing, big tumbling drowned trees could be below the surface of the river turning like the fabled octopus with grasping arms.

Once again they had to make a crossing on their own and once again he loosed Pasha and the little mare Fancy plunged in. She fought across the current, they drifted down, Johanna clutched up her skirts and prepared to jump but they made it.

On the far side they were on the Lampasas Road and would miss Meridian altogether. That was all right. They would soon come to Durand which was larger and had more people, all of them with money in their pockets he sincerely hoped.

A brief rain; again it was a wet world where each leaf of the live oak, clinging to the twigs throughout the winter, held a drop at its tip. The live oaks never lost their leaves in the winter; he had seen them standing green in a snowfall.

Johanna bent her head far back to look up into the leafy canopy and the rainy sky. There was a cautious wonder on her face. She said something in Kiowa in a low voice. So much water, such giant trees, each possessing a spirit. Drops like jewels cascaded from their spidery hands.

He said, Tree. He took off his old broad-brimmed field hat and ran his hand through his hair, which was as fine as cobweb and as white. Put the hat back on.

Yes, tlee, tlee.

He pointed out: Pine. Oak. Cedar. First the general class and then the specific.

Yes, Kep-den Kidd.

As they drove, he pointed back to Pasha, to his nose, to the bacon. She seemed to have had some acquaintance with the English language before. Maybe her memory just needed a jog. She said, Hoas, nos-ah, bekkin. Then he rose to his feet. Stend up, she said. He sat down. Sit don. *Kontah*, sit don.

Captain Kidd was fairly sure *Kontah* meant grandfather but whether this was an honorific or a slang term he had no way of knowing.

He said, *Kontah, Opa.*

Yes yes, *Kontah Opa*!

Opa, German for grandfather. Well, they were getting somewhere. The word *Opa* clicked into some otherwise disengaged gear in her mind. Then she became interested in the puzzle of another language, other words, other grammars. She thought for a moment and then said, *Cho-henna clepp honts.* She clapped her hands. *Cho-henna laff-a.* She came out with a hearty false laugh, bouncing around on the wagon seat. Then she held up her hands with the fingers spread. Wan, doo, tlee, foh, fife, siss, sefen, ate-ah, nine-ah, den.

The mouse ran up the clock, he said, and when he saw the dubious look on her face, her anxious need to understand, he patted her hand. It is all right, he said.

Allite.

She could not pronounce either the German *R* nor the English *R* or one of the two *th* sounds and perhaps never would. Lain, she said. Watah, plenty good much watah, plenty lain.

Excellent, Johanna! Excellent.

Hmmm hmmm hmmm, she hummed to herself and rocked back and forth and then busied herself with tearing off the remains of the lace edging on her dress. She had begun it when she tied up her braid during the fight on the Brazos and had decided to finish the job.

As long as they were traveling she was content and happy and the world held great interest for her but Captain Kidd wondered what would happen when she found she was never to wander over the face of the earth again, when she was to be confined forever to her Leonberger relatives in a square house that could not be broken down and packed on a travois. He had a failing feeling around his heart when he thought of it. Cynthia Parker had starved herself to death when she was returned to her white relatives. So had Temple Friend. Other returned captives had become alcoholics, solitaries, strange people. They were all odd, the returned captives. All peculiar with minds oddly formed, never quite one thing or another. As Doris had said back in Spanish Fort, all those captured as children and returned were restless and hungry for some spiritual solace, abandoned by two cultures, dark shooting stars lost in the outer heavens.

And could he abandon her now to her relatives, after they had saved each other's lives, after the battle they had fought? He had to. They were her blood kin. This was a painful thought but he had had enough of anxiety for a good long while and so he turned his mind back to the here and now.

In Durand he would have to give a reading of the latest news since they had shot up nearly all their money. The Captain's previous funds had been destroyed by the War Between the States and several minor debts in property taxes, but minor or not they were debts and by 1866 his deposits and bank stocks were all gone. The local San Antonio Commission for the Support of the Confederacy had threatened him with jail if he would not invest in Confederate bonds and so there it all went. He sold his printing business and paid his debts and took to the road. Maria had died the year before, and it was as if some tether had been loosed, the anchor rope of a hot-air balloon cut free and the Captain rose up and sailed away on the winds of chance. He was nearly seventy-two now and his finest possessions were his gold hunting watch and Pasha and his reading voice.

Cho-henna estomp *choo*! She lifted her bare foot and pointed to it and then stamped it on the floorboards.

Not shoe, *foot,* he said. He reached back and found one of her shoes. He held it up; a black and confining laced thing with a blunt toe and a one-inch heel. The laces were missing. She had used them for something. Shoe, he said. He pointed to her foot. Foot!

Fery well, Cho-henna stomp *foot*! Cho-henna weff hont! She waved her hand. Kep-dun stend up! He stood up. Kep-dun sit don! He sat down. Kep-dun clepp honts! He wearily clapped his hands. Kep-dun laff!

No, he said.

Ah ah ah, Kep-dun, pliss!

All right. He managed to raise a false and hearty laugh. Ha! Ha! Ha! Now, that's enough for today.

This made her fall into helpless laughter. Then she cried, Kep-dun heat blek-fass, Cho-henna choot gun (shooting noise), hoas tlot, Kep-dun choot gun (shooting noise again), Wan, doo, tlee, foh, fife, siss, sefen, ate-ah, nine-ah, den.

Very good, my dear, now let's be quiet. I am elderly and frail and my nerves fray easily. His scalp still had the running galvanized crawl of pain and his right eyebrow probably needed stitches but was not going to get them.

Fery good lain, hoas choot gun ha ha ha! Hoas eat blek-fass! Hoas laff! (Here an imitation whinny) and she klepped her honts and laughed again and so they went on down the Lampasas Road through the trees, toward Durand on the Bosque River, with the Kiowa captive girl inventing new and even more improbable sentences and the Captain's eyes watering with pain.

Wan foot, doo foots, wan hont, doo honts, doo hoas, big hoas, lidda hoas . . .

Johanna, *shut up*.

Cho-henna chut *up*!

As they came within a mile of Durand through the dripping forest of live oaks he saw men riding toward him. He put one hand out to Johanna. She stopped. She became perfectly silent. The men who rode toward them wore ragged clothing and shabby hats but they were well-armed. They had spent all their money on revolvers and the new repeating short-barreled carbines. Spencers, gleaming new.

The sun had come out and the noon light outlined the men as they rode toward the Captain's wagon. They sparkled with falling drops from the leaves, shake-down showers. The Captain pulled up. He gazed at them with a steady and unperturbed expression. Behind it he wondered if they had somehow got word of the Great Brazos Ten-Cent Shoot-Out.

He wondered what they wanted. Where they were from. There was anarchy in Texas in 1870 and every man did what was right in his own eyes.

One of the men with a trimmed black beard came up

alongside the light spring wagon, on the Captain's side, and his cavalry stirrup with its blunt tapadero made chunking noises against the stopped fore wheel. He looked down at them, at the cut over the Captain's eye and the spots of blood on his shirt and the muddied wagon spokes. An old man and a girl. The girl had sunk down behind the canted dashboard and only her dirty fingers gripping the wood and her face were visible. The man on horseback was dark-skinned and black-eyed but this did not matter to Johanna, native Americans looked not at the color of skin but at the intentions, the body posture, the language of hands. That was how they stayed alive. Johanna fixed him like a print in her suspicious blue gaze.

Curative Waters, eh? He regarded the gold lettering on the sides.

I bought it from the proprietor, said Captain Kidd, who went bust. He kept his voice within the range of reasonable tones. He had the girl to think about.

Did it have the bullet holes in it already?

Yes, as a matter of fact it did, said the Captain. He tried to straighten out the wavy brim of his old hat. He had two days' growth of sparkling white beard and knew he looked like a derelict but he sat straight-backed and tall in his canvas coat and fixed in his mind the revolver on his left on the floorboards under the bacon. He said, It came fully supplied with bullet holes.

Very curious. And so, where are you headed? said the black-bearded man. His voice was low and rasping.

Captain Kidd thought about it for a moment and decided to answer him. The scarves of smoke were coming from a campfire, one most likely belonging to these men, nearby, hidden.

Durand, the Captain said.

That your final destination?

No.

So where, then?

Castroville.

Where's that?

Fifteen miles west of San Antonio.

That's a long piece of travel.

The temptation was great to say *Why is it your concern, you filthy ignorant brigand,* but he looked down at the girl and smiled his creased smile and patted her inflexible white fingers seized on the dashboard.

He said, This girl was a captive of the Kiowa, lately rescued, and I am returning her to her relatives there.

The savages, the man said. He regarded the child, her hair stiff with dirt, skinned knuckles, and a dress smeared with dirt and charcoal and bacon grease where she had wiped her hands. He shook his head. Why they go and steal children I will never understand. Do they not have ary of their own?

I am as mystified as you are, said the Captain.

The black-bearded man said, And the Indians know as much about soap as a hog knows about Sunday. Miss? he said. Look here.

He fished in the watch pocket of his jeans and found a lump of saltwater taffy thick with lint. He held it out, bent from his saddle, smiling. Quick as a snake she struck it from his hand and dropped farther down behind the dashboard.

Ah. The man nodded. They come back wild. I have heard about this.

The others had ridden around the wagon. They sat loose and easy in their worn dragoon saddles and did not bother to unlimber either revolver or carbine. Clearly Johanna and the Captain were harmless.

The Captain then understood they had not heard of the Great Brazos Ten-Cent Shoot-Out at Carlyle Springs. It was two days behind but a good bet was that these men did not travel much beyond this area. As yet there was almost no telegraph service in most of Texas.

Who you for? The black-bearded man turned to the Captain. His manner had changed. Who'd you vote for? Davis or Hamilton?

The Captain now knew that disaster awaited any reading of the news in Durand, but they had shot themselves into poverty and had a long way to go. The only other thing he could think of to do was to sell the wagon and proceed on horseback. But his back and his hip joints were not strong anymore and long distances on horseback had become increasingly painful.

He said, I am deeply offended that you would dare to ask who I voted for. We are guaranteed a secret vote. I am a veteran of Horseshoe Bend and Resaca de la Palma and I did not fight to establish a sleazy South American dictatorship. I fought for the rights of freeborn Englishmen.

There. That should confuse them.

I see. The black-bearded man thought about it. Are you English?

No, I am not.

Then this is not making sense, here.

Never mind that, Captain Kidd said. Are you stopping me in some kind of official capacity? I am about to lose my patience.

One of the others in a hat with a very tall crown said, Nobody who voted for Davis is getting into Erath County.

Is this an official decision by the local administration?

The black-bearded man smiled. He said, Sir, there isn't any local administration. There isn't any sheriff. Davis's men turfed him out. There isn't any JP, there isn't any mayor, there aren't any commissioners. Davis and the U.S. Army threw them out. They all had been in the Confederate Army or they were public servants under the Confederacy and so that was it for them. But he won't send anybody to replace them. So we took on the job. You are accountable to us.

Captain Kidd glanced down at Johanna, who listened intently with her eyes blue and wide. He patted her fingers. For how much?

A long pause.

Ah, just give us a half-dollar.

FOURTEEN

THEY PULLED INTO the loading yard of a big broom and stave mill at the edge of the Bosque River. There were cottonwoods along the river and their tiny new leaves shivered even without a wind and dripped rainwater in pinhead glitters. It was the first cottonwoods he had seen in a long time. The Bosque was shallow and they had no trouble with the crossing.

The undershot wheel that powered the machines turned and brought up bright squares of water and spilled them into the river. A man looked up from his binding work. He sat beside a broom-making machine amid a heaping of broom-corn sheaves. A pile of handles lay nearby. He and his brooms were in a big cavernous building, open on the sides, with a shingle roof. It gave some protection from the sun and rain. The sky was laddered with passing waves of low clouds. Chickens stalked around and surveyed their world with calm yellow eyes.

The Captain asked if they could shelter here for the night.

The man said, They's a hotel.

I see, said Captain Kidd. But I can't afford one right now.

They's a wagon yard.

It seems safer here. I have this child, you see. I can offer fifteen cents for the night. The Captain leaned forward and fixed the man in his old hawk's gaze.

I ain't that hard up.

How hard up are you?

Fifty cents. You'll want to use the pump and give your horses some forage, plus these wood scraps to cook with and some of my straw to sleep on.

Good God, said Kidd. And cotton's going begging for seventeen cents the pound.

I ain't buying no cotton.

Captain Kidd turned to Johanna. My dear, he said. Five dime-ah.

She dived into the shot box and found a shotgun shell, broke it open, and poured out the money.

CAPTAIN KIDD WASHED up as best he could, tapped the cut over his eye with a wet cloth. He dusted it again with the gray wound powder. Then he tried to show Johanna on the hands of his watch when he would be back. She stared at the dial face intently and put her fingertip on the crystal, first over the hour hand and then the minute hand, and her eyes moved as she watched the second hand jumping forward like an insect.

Time, he said. Two o'clock.

Time, *Kontah.*

When the little hand is at three, I will be back.

Then he put it in her palm. He was almost persuaded that she understood.

Then he dropped more coins in the pocket of his old canvas

coat and walked into town. The edges of his coat pockets were dark with grime. Soon he would have to throw the coat away and get another. When he was rich. Durand had a main street and board sidewalks. Otherwise the town was scattered out among the woods and the little rises. Cottonwood catkins had burst and the silky cotton was drifting down the street and piling up in the corners of anything and anywhere.

First he arranged for a reading space at the new mercantile building. It was very long and narrow, with glass cases full of knives, china shepherdesses, and silverware and handkerchiefs. On the walls were shelves of shirts and suspenders. Farther back were readymade shoes and boots, work jackets and bolts of cloth. The men's and ladies' underclothing were no doubt hidden below the counters. It would do. The man accepted his dollar in coins.

He put up the handbills everywhere and was followed by urchins in galluses and straw hats, some with shoes, up and down the dirt streets of Durand. The Captain said to leave him alone or he would twist their noses. He asked the tallest boy if he could read the bill.

I could if I wanted to, the boy said. But I don't care to.

A man of independent thought, said the Captain. It says I am going to saw a woman in half tonight. A fat woman.

They hung back with dubious looks and he walked on.

He tacked his bills up at the livery stable, the school, the Feed and Provisions for Man and Beast, the wool warehouse, the post yard piled high with cedar posts, at the wagon maker's, and at the leather repair. He handed one to a man in a black sack coat and a vest and a pair of modest side-button black shoes.

The man carried a gold-headed cane. He glanced down at the Captain's riding boots. They were well-made and showed it.

Very good, the man said, and lifted his hat. He read the bill. News. We have so little of it. Are you come from Dallas?

I am.

And what are the conditions there with the Davis appointees?

Captain Kidd sensed danger but he had no choice but to plunge on. I have no idea, he said. I merely bought my newspapers, the latest come from the East.

So you will read from the *Daily State Journal*?

I will not. It is mere propaganda.

Sir!

It is opinion only. I refuse to be an unpaid mouthpiece for the powers in Austin. Captain Kidd could not make himself back down, it was not a thing for which he had any aptitude, nor had he ever, and it was far too late in life to change. He said, So understand this; I read of events. Events from places far removed so that, indeed, they have a fairy-tale quality about them and if you do not care for that sort of thing then stay home. He stood over the man at his full height, dignified in his threadbare duck coat and his disreputable traveling hat.

The man said, I am Dr. Beavis, Anthony Beavis, and I do not consider the *Daily State Journal* to be composed of fairy tales. It is in fact a valuable contribution to the current debates.

I didn't say it was full of fairy tales, Doctor. Captain Kidd lifted his hat. If only it were. Good day to you, sir.

AT THE BROOM and stave mill Johanna had busied herself with domestic chores. The man making brooms stared with narrow eyes at the blankets strung on lines and the harnesses flung over the gunnels of the wagon and the black beans and bacon simmering on the tiny stove. He regarded the *Curative Waters* gold lettering and the bullet holes with serious doubt. He said that the girl had taken the horses out to graze along the banks of the Bosque.

There's something wrong with that girl, he said.

And what would that be? said Captain Kidd. He sat on the tailgate with his stack of newspapers beside him and a flat carpenter's pencil. He decided on different articles from the ones he had read in Dallas. Something more soothing. He had the AP sheets with news of floods along the Susquehanna and railroad bonds being passed in Illinois to fund the Burlington and Illinois Central. Surely no one could object to railroads per se. He had his *London Times* and the *New-York Evening Post*, the *Philadelphia Inquirer*, *Milwaukee Daily News* (the "Cheese and Norwegian Tatler" as Captain Kidd called it), *Harper's Weekly*. He had *Blackwood's*, and then of course *Household Words*, out of date but good for any time, any place. None of them mentioned Hamilton or Davis or Negro suffrage in Texas or the military occupation or the Peace Policy.

Captain Kidd hoped to get out of Durand with his finances refreshed and an unperforated skin. He had to. Johanna had no one else but himself. Nothing between her and this cross-grained contentious white man's world that she would never understand. Captain Kidd looked up and enviously considered the chickens—so daft, so stupid, so uninformed.

Well, for one thing, she don't speak English.

The man had a broom handle socketed into the hub of the

machine and he rotated it as he tied on wet bunches of broom corn. The fool sat there and did that all day long and probably considered himself an expert on the English language because it spilled out of his mouth like water from an undershot brain and he didn't even have to think about it.

So?

Well. She looks English.

Do tell.

Captain Kidd drew thick lines around various articles in the *Inquirer.* Must be careful here. Philadelphia meant Quakers and Quakers meant the Peace Policy, which was getting people killed in North Texas and even down this far south of the Red. He chose a daintily written fluff piece about ice-skating on Lemon Hill, a spot apparently somewhere on the edge of Philadelphia. *Here, read and believe, they are building bonfires on this ice and ladies are skating about on it, their hoop skirts swaying. They are safe and life is quiet, the ice is firm and holds them up above the sinister and lethal depths.*

Well, what is she, then?

The man's face was broad and low, like a soup tureen. Hens pecked at his feet. Here Penelope, here Amelia, he said, in sweet inviting tones. He held down his hand and the hens pecked broom-corn seeds from it. Captain Kidd looked up in irritation. He was trying to care for a semi-savage girl child and fend off criminals who would kidnap her for the most dreadful purposes and at the same time make enough money in the only way he knew how so they might eat and travel and on top of that evade the brutal political clashes of Texans. A tall order.

Why don't you just shut the hell up and tend to your brooms?

Kidd said. I haven't asked you for your mother's maiden name, have I?

Listen here, the man said.

Spare me, said the Captain.

He opened *Blackwood's*. He closed his eyes briefly and asked for calm. Then from beyond the rail fence that enclosed one end of the stave mill yard he heard shouts and shrieks. He closed his eyes again. What now, what now. It was Johanna's particular Kiowa high-pitched continuous stream of tonal words and a woman shouting in English. It came from the direction of the Bosque River. He threw down the carpenter's pencil and grabbed a blanket, for he had some idea of what might be happening.

Johanna was in the shallows among the Carrizo cane, naked except for the tattered old corset and sagging drawers one of the ladies in Wichita Falls had given her. A woman with a wooden bucket in one hand was chasing her. They ran over the stones and shallow places, both of them spewing water. Johanna flung herself into a deep hole at the lip of a small rapids, screaming at the woman. Her wet hair was in dark ropes over her face and you could see the row of white bottom teeth as she yelled. She was calling down the dark magic of her guardian spirit upon the woman and if she had had the kitchen knife in her hand she would have stuck it in this good woman of Durand.

We cannot have this! the woman cried. She stood up to her knees in the current and her dress skirts billowed up with trapped air. She was young and properly attired and outraged. We cannot have naked bathing here! She jerked off her bonnet and beat it on her thigh in frustration. The big live oaks lifted and sighed in exasperated sounds and from the town came the sound of choral singing—Wednesday, choir practice.

Ma'am, said Captain Kidd. He saw the wedding ring. Please. She was merely bathing.

In public! The young woman cried. Unclothed!

Not entirely, said Captain Kidd. He waded into the shallows of the Bosque, boots and all, and threw the blanket around the girl. Calm yourself, he said. She doesn't know any better.

Across the river was the wagon yard, where the freighters camped, and several of the drivers had come to stand and watch and lean on their wagon boxes. Leaf shadows like laughter ran over their faces.

Captain Kidd said, She was a captive. An Indian captive.

We can't have this, said the young woman. She held on to the rope bucket handle with both hands. I don't care if she's a Hottentot. I don't care if she's Lola Montez. She was parading her charms out there in the river like a Dallas huzzy.

Captain Kidd led Johanna out of the water. He said, I am returning her to her people by contract with the Indian Agent Samuel Hammond of Fort Sill. Official government business, Department of War.

Johanna sobbed and leaned against him, ankle deep in the green water of the Bosque. He said, Torn cruelly from her mother's arms at the tender age of six, her mother brained before her eyes, starved and beaten, she has even forgotten her own language and the proper modesty of civilized peoples. Her sufferings were beyond description.

The young woman paused, then fell silent. Finally she said,

Well. But she must be corrected. She must have this forcefully impressed upon her. About modesty while bathing.

Johanna put her hands over her eyes. She could think only of her Kiowa mother, Three Spotted, her mother's laughter and how they had all dunked each other in the clear water of Cache Creek in the Wichita Mountains, and screamed and fell backward straight into the water, and far up the mountainside a group of young men drummed for the fun of it. They had waded and splashed down the clear currents, four, five girls with strings of vermilion beads in their hair. She wept for them and for those mountains, a strange adult weeping with open hands and a bowed head. For all her terrible losses, which of a sudden had come back to her in a painful wounding rush.

Well, I am sorry to hear it, said the young woman. Her voice grew softer. And then after a moment she bent to Johanna and said, My dear, I am very sorry.

Leave her alone, said the Captain in a stiff voice. He lifted his hat to the young woman and took Johanna's hand. And if you were to call yourself a Christian you would find shoes and clothing for this girl, to supply her on her journey.

They returned to the wagon, his boots full of water making squidging noises, Johanna a dripping wad of coarse blanket and wet drawers bunched in her hands, barefoot, hurt, angry, despairing.

BY EIGHT O'CLOCK it was dark in Durand and he made sure she was bedded down in the wagon and in her nightgown and the lantern lit. She hummed a slow and comforting song to herself and sat wrapped in the *jorongo,* for which she had developed a strong attachment, and took up the task of sewing up the frayed edge of the gray wool blanket. She had put his blood-spotted shirt to soak in salty water. The Captain went back to one of the stalls and pulled off his boots and spurs, changed into his reading clothes, put on the black lace-ups, and shaved.

Bekkin, she looked up when he walked out. *Haina bekkin.*

How very astute of you, he said. I am, in fact, going to bring home the bacon. He put his portfolio under his arm. I will astound the citizens with my informative readings concerning the Hottentots and Lola Montez and the Illinois railroads. They will pour out both silver and gold at my feet and we will have not only bekkin but eggs. How about that? First thing tomorrow we will patronize the local establishments.

He bent his head and regarded her with concern and some tenderness. It seemed his small warrior burst so easily into tears from time to time and was soon afterward bright with energy and laughter. So it was with children. May she always be so. He arranged his black ascot and shot his cuffs. She nodded and sewed and raised her dusty blond eyebrows a fraction as the gesture of a smile. Her freckles looked dark in the lantern light.

He would have liked to kiss her on the cheek but he had no idea if the Kiowas kissed one another or if so, did grandfathers kiss granddaughters. You never knew. Cultures were mine fields.

He patted the air with a gentle motion.

Sit. Stay.

FIFTEEN

———•◦•———

THE MERCANTILE FILLED up early. A U.S. Army soldier stood outside the door and required each man to open his coat and show he was not carrying a handgun. Some were. They were illegal but the sergeant said nothing, only gestured toward a bench. By the time the Mercantile was filled there were seven or eight revolvers and one little two-shot Sneaky Pete on the bench.

Men and some women sat in stiff-backed wooden chairs or stood leaning on the counters and were prevented from slouching against the glass cases by J. D. Allan, Proprietor. Captain Kidd did not stand searching the faces of the crowd but he saw them nonetheless at the edge of his vision. He laid out his newspapers and the AP wire sheets. He saw how they divided themselves, one group from another, and stared at each other with looks like warning flares. They sat and leaned and smoked, hatless among the articles of mechanical manufacture sent from far places. There were boots and shoes and suspenders and hair dye and buttons and ironstone plates from England. Kerosene lamps with green shades hung swaying from overhead chains and in the distance thunder came toward them with threatening rumbles. The storm was coming from far beyond the hundredth meridian.

He began as always with his greetings to the establishment of the town and a brief comment on the roads. People always liked to hear about the condition of the roads from travelers. The Captain said the roads along the Red were all good, he did not know about the Little Wichita, he had crossed it more than a week ago but it might be up again. The Brazos ferry was not operating; washed away perhaps, but the landings on both sides were good. The road from the Brazos to here was in good condition. He paused and with one veined hand flattened his papers, waiting to hear if anyone would mention an altercation there involving firearms, but that was not what was on the minds of several of his listeners.

A hatless man stood up and cried, When Davis gets done there'll be a paved road to the house of ever damn one of his cronies in the legislature!

The Captain's head came up.

Silence!!

He had a very strong voice for a man his age, and he was over six feet tall and imposing in his crow-black clothes and his angry dark eyes, his brilliant moon-silver hair. His reading glasses flashed with gold rims as he stared around at his audience. The long narrow room smelled of trouble. He said, Sir, the people here assembled did not pay good money to come and sit here and listen to your complaints. I would suspect they have heard them before.

Laughter.

Captain Kidd cleared his throat, pressed back his glasses,

and brought out the *Inquirer* to read of Lemon Hill. He slid out pages of the *Tribune* and its news of railroads, reading steadily, reading like a broom-making machine and sweeping all before him except for a man who called out,

Why don't you read from the Houston *Tri-Weekly Union,* sir?

Another man rose to his feet. Because that's a damned Davis paper, and they are every one of them damned unreconstructed thieves!

They are Republicans! Loyal to the Union to a man!

Another man yelled, And so what then? They have become indoctrinated by professional agitators!

Gentlemen! Captain Kidd shouted.

A grudging silence and the three men standing sat down slowly and glared at one another.

He did not have very long. He read quickly, flipping newsprint, read of far places and frozen climes, of reports of revolution in Chile, trying to bring them distant magic that was not only marvelous but true. He read of riots in the Punjab re: census taking, female privacy; all the spilling images of a rumored world weighted with railroads and modernity coming up against ancient tribal hatreds.

The tulip—he read quickly—long under guard in Turkey for years—bulbs confiscated from diplomatic pouches—now superseded in value by the Angora goat from the region of Ankara—Pashas object—Angoras smuggled aboard the *Highland Star*...

Davis will shut down the *Dallas Courier* under the Printing Bill! a little blond man screamed. Two hundred thousand dollars of tax money to hand out to radical newspapers!

Two men got to their feet and came face-to-face shouting about the turncoat Hamilton and the corrupt Davis, others tried to separate them but they were intent on doing each other damage and the people separating them, each with a bottom lip stuck out and bent backward trying to avoid blows, became involved in the passions expressed. Women seized their skirts in both hands and got out of the building and several picked up their husbands' or fathers' or brothers' handguns from the bench outside and carried them away. The U.S. Army sergeant listened for a moment to the shouts about military rule and Austin corruption and the Printing Bill and stayed where he was.

Finally it came to fists and chairs and the rainstorm came merrily on as one of the glass cases splintered. The coin can was turned over and men trod on the money. The hanging kerosene lanterns swung back and forth and people trampled the chairs down and shook the walls. One man broke a good Wedgwood commemorative plate over another's head. A short man pulled off his belt and began laying about him with the buckle. At the end, the two major combatants, who were the owner of the hotel and the schoolteacher, a young man with spiky, ill-cut hair and pale cheeks inflamed with acne but a determined fighter, struck and twisted themselves out of the door and into the street.

All the rest followed.

CAPTAIN KIDD REMAINED for a few moments at the lectern. He put his chin on his fist and surveyed the wreckage. Then he folded his newspapers and put them in the portfolio and let out a long breath. It was much better up on the Red River, he decided, where all you really had to deal with was the Comanche, the Kiowa, and sometimes the U.S. Army.

And up there in North Texas, of course, was Mrs. Gannet.

He walked through the overturned chairs and saw all the silver coins flung about on the floorboards, glinting like eyes. It was humiliating but he would have to grovel on his hands and knees and pick them all up. He would not have done it had it not been for Johanna. He would have said, *You blustering loudmouthed jackasses can have them* and he would have walked away.

The Army sergeant at the door was gone. Fat raindrops spattered out on the dirt street. Men were out there still shouting at one another with the intermittent voices of peacemakers crying *Listen, listen now* . . . The Captain knelt down and began collecting the coins.

Here, sir, you shouldn't have to do that.

It was the man with the short black beard who had stopped him on the road.

No, I shouldn't, said Captain Kidd. But here I am doing it.

The man drew up an unbroken chair for him and indicated it with a sweep of the hand. The Captain sat down gratefully, his hip joints aflame, and the man began to pick up all the coins himself.

My name is John Calley, the man said. He poured coins back into the can out of his large, callused hand. He said, We should not have taken your money this morning on the road. I am regretting it.

The Captain nodded and pressed his fingertips against his eyes. He said, You have fallen in with bad company.

That would be my cousins and my brother.

Still.

Well, yes.

Captain Kidd thought about the apparent ages of the man's companions, cousins and brother, and said, They were in the war.

So was I.

Ah, said Kidd. You were young.

No sir, I was seventeen.

That's young.

The Captain had forgotten he himself had seen his sixteenth birthday at the Battle of Horseshoe Bend, firing at the Red Sticks with a rifled Kentucky long bore. He watched the coins drop into the paint can, one after another.

He said, You should abandon your wayward relatives and decline their illegal activities.

No telling what's illegal these days. John Calley stepped forward to the shelves of suspenders and the collar buttons on cards. He was now dressed in pressed dark trousers and a cutaway, a snowy white shirt with a high collar and a cravat. It was all somewhat frayed but clean. His dark beard was shorter, neatly trimmed. He wore good boots, the Captain saw, with a pair of arm-and-hand spurs. Calley peered at the shelf and said, Well, be damned, there's one up here. He picked the ten-cent piece up in his thick fingers, delicately. Then he said, Of course I should. But things change week to week. He poured the money out of his fist into the can. The legal situation is very unstable. Land titles, everything.

The Captain realized that John Calley had come in his best clothes to show the Captain that he was not, indeed, a filthy ignorant brigand but a man gently reared. A serious man. That he wanted the Captain's respect.

The Captain cleaned his glasses slowly on his handkerchief. You are not thinking of reading law, are you? he said.

Oh God no! John Calley stood holding the paint can. I am looking for honest work.

That's an improvement, then, from when I first came upon you.

Granted. Calley flushed a bit at the cheekbones. And so if one were to read law, where is there solid ground? Somewhere there has to be a bedrock of the law.

Captain Kidd said, It has been said by authorities that the law should apply the same to the king and to the peasant both, it should be written out and placed in the city square for all to see, it should be written simply and in the language of the common people, lest the people grow weary of their burdens.

The young man tipped his head toward the Captain with an odd look on his face. It was a kind of longing, a kind of hope.

Who said that?

Hammurabi.

CAPTAIN KIDD KNEW the best thing would be to leave immediately, in the night, as they had done before. Same situation as Dallas. He had collected his fees for the reading but yet none of the establishments of Durand were open and if he were to pound on the door of J. D. Allan, Prop., to ask to purchase .38 ammunition it would become known and the general condition of suspicion would have it that he was on his way to shoot someone of the opposite party, whatever party that was. He had eight bullets left for the revolver, and the dove shot and several pounds of gun-powder and a supply of dimes. That would have to do.

From the banks of the Bosque, by the dim light of the candle lantern, he collected Pasha and Fancy. The rain had lessened but still it dripped from his hat brim and his silk topper had become heavy with it and sat on his head in a damp chunk. He slogged through the wet grass calling to the horses in a low voice. Little Fancy seemed to delight in her musical bell and lifted her head and jingled it. The horses were rested and full of new spring grass. He led them in. Inside the stave mill he changed to his old traveling clothes by the light of the lantern. He wondered how many candles they had left. The silence and the lacy patterns that the candle threw out of the intricately pierced tin shade were comforting. He ate a quick meal of black beans and bacon.

He called softly, Johanna, Johanna.

Kep-den!

She jumped out of the wagon bed, throwing aside her blankets in a dramatic gesture. She was in her nightgown with hay in her hair and a looping tangle of fabrics and textiles in her hands. Looka here, y'all, she said.

The Captain turned to her with a smile. She had not yet distinguished the second person plural from the singular but every day saw an improvement.

Shhh, he said. What?

I dress-a, I chekkit, I drawers, I stokkin! Kep-den, look! She held out a bar of soap.

Shhh, yes, excellent. Who gave you this?

She laid all her secondhand clothes in a neat pile on the tailgate and gazed at them happily. Bad water lady, she said.

Good, good, now go dress, we have to leave.

So the young woman who tried to drag Johanna from the Bosque had been stricken with Christian conscience and had collected clothing for the girl; a dress in yellow and madder carriage check, a jacket of dark green, drawers, stockings, and soap. He ran the hems and edges through his fingers, looked at all the buttons; sewed secure and tight. Clothing was hard to come by and these were all of top quality. Good. Stricken consciences are an excellent thing, all told. The girl now had three dresses and plenty of underthings. She would not have to meet her relatives dirty and ill-clad. The thought gave him a small, sharp pain in his heart.

The rainstorm had all but passed over. Now the sky was clearing. He put the horse's hobbles in his old chore coat pocket and in the stave-mill yard he backed Fancy between the shafts and threw the harness over her back. The gold letters shone in the moonlight.

Johanna ducked into the shed row and came carrying, at the last, something wrapped in burlap but the Captain was too hurried to think about it and so blew out the candle lantern, stepped up to the driver's seat, turned the little roan mare and the light spring wagon with its screeching fifth wheel. They moved quietly out of arguing, fighting, contentious Durand and into the dark of an early spring Texas night while overhead nightjars moved and sang their low and throaty songs. They swept low, like owls, and carried the light of the stars on their backs. On down the white moonlit road at a steady trot, seven miles an hour, bang bang bang, Pasha trotting behind, eleven at night when all decent folks were in bed. The Captain was not sure what came next, what town, what county, what new trouble.

Johanna climbed over the backrest and took up the burlap bundle and returned to the driver's seat beside the Captain. She sat beside him and opened it.

Blek-fass! she cried.

Oh no, Johanna, no.

Two chicken carcasses with bloody feathers and no heads lay in her lap. It was Penelope and Amelia. Dead. Deader than John Wilkes Booth. She smiled down at them. She had twisted their heads off and gutted them and out of the cavity of one she held up the quivering blob of an unlaid egg which she had saved out of the entrails.

Is good! she said. She patted his arm with a sticky hand. Blek-fass.

He drove for a few moments with his eyes shut.

It was too late to go back and pay the disagreeable broom man. Too late to apologize, too late to leave money to reimburse the peevish creature. The Captain was now probably thought of in Durand not only as a Davis man but a common chicken thief. He was not sure which was worse. The Captain's hand went to his forehead. A dreadful loss of status in the world. In his world. Loss of reputation and the regard of our fellow persons is in any society, from Iceland to East Indies, a terrible blow to the spirit. It is worse than being penniless and more cutting than the blades of enemies.

The Captain said, in an even voice, into which he managed to inject a tone of delight, Indeed! Clever child! Now we have breakfast.

The night was cold and he felt it in his bones and the cool streaks on his cheeks. He realized they were tears, for the trouble that lay ahead of her. For all the years of roofs and walls and the peculiar rules against stealing chickens. He was still tired. He was still drained. She was busy wrapping up the carcasses and singing. She had not the slightest notion of animals as private property, except for horses. Horses belonged to one person, everything else was dinner at large. She would not hesitate to put a bullet through a calf or a kid. In his imagination he saw her walking into the Leonberger yard triumphantly dragging a headless prize foal to please her stranger relatives.

She raised her head and saw him shouldering away the tears on his cheeks.

Oh Kep-dun, she said in a falling tone. She reached up and stroked away the tears with her hard and callused fingertips. Her fingers were gummy with blood and there were down feathers stuck on them. One drifted down in the moonlight like a falling minute angel onto his coat.

Leave me alone, Johanna.

Hungli, she said in a decisive tone. *Kontah* hungli.

Grandfather was hungry, that was what was wrong, he was hungry and she would soon have him fixed up with roasted chicken with an egg cooked in the rib cage.

He said, Old people cry easily, my dear. One of the afflictions of age.

You-all hungli. She patted the hen's corpse with a hearty feathered sound. Is all lite Cho-henna?

Yes, he said. It's all right.

SIXTEEN

———•◆•———

THEY WENT DOWN the road, which was now the Lampasas Road with Durand somewhere behind them, and the sun came up bloody red in a clearing sky. The country was high and flat with only an occasional shift in the landscape. They were exposed. They were the only thing moving in all that horizontal world. They came to Cranfills Gap and stayed the night on the Leon River at a campsite that looked as if it were frequented by convoys of freight wagons. He hoped some would pull in so he could ask for news of Britt but none came, there were only the deep narrow tire tracks and flat spaces in the dirt where somebody had thrown out a bucket of dishwater, a dead campfire. They turned the horses out to find what new grass they could, though the freighters' teams had nearly eaten it all up.

There he had his roasted chicken and slept heavily. He dreamed of an armed man in the shadows that had about him some terrible noxious smell, and then the man was rising out of the Leon River, amphibious and not entirely human. The Captain sat upright and grasped the coat where his revolver was wrapped but waited it out. This always happened to him when there had been some conflict. First on the Brazos and then Durand. The dreams had just caught up with him now. He knew them of old. Maria Luisa had learned to slide out of bed and stand several feet away and say, over and over, Jeff. Jeff. *Querido*. Jeff. And he would come out of an intensely real dream where he was fighting for his life, sometimes at Resaca, sometimes on the Tallapoosa, sometimes in broken streets that appeared to be a bombed city with house-to-house fighting as it had been in Monterrey.

Perhaps it was something like this that changed the captive children forever; the violence they had endured when they were captured, their parents killed. Perhaps it sank down in their young minds and stayed there, invisible and unacknowledged but very powerful.

He had no one to awaken him now in a soft voice. He let go of his rolled coat and closed his eyes and quieted himself and lay back down and slept again.

All the next day they stayed in camp and he slept most of it away under the awning. Then they drove into Cranfills Gap with its one store and bought supplies and a little twenty-five-gallon water butt, filled it and went on.

They made twenty miles the next day, a very commendable day's travel. It was because the road was flat and the surface of a good sandy consistency and Fancy was well-rested. The Captain felt much better. Their English lessons continued. She could now count to a hundred and lace her shoes, when he could convince her to wear them, and sing the first verse of "Hard Times." She could tell the hour and the minute hands on his watch. She was full of roast chicken and energy. Time,

Kontah! Is time, is time. She stood up on the driver's seat and did the Rabbit Dance, the Kiowa children's dance, and when he finally told her to quit it, she jumped down and ran alongside and found the lid of a tin of salve with a bee impressed on it and so made buzzing noises as she flew it up and down.

They passed only two farm wagons and another company of cavalry in all that way. The cavalrymen were being moved from San Antonio to Fort Sill and the major reminded the Captain to be careful. There were raiders, he said, in the hill country.

Then why don't you do something about them? the Captain said.

I am under orders, sir. We don't just go wandering about and do whatever we like. The major pressed his heels to his horse and rode on. Johanna sat quietly in the back and watched after them as they went on north.

They camped near the town of Langford Cove and he felt entirely recovered.

At Lampasas was a great good spring of water. He had passed by there several times. It would be a good place to shake out their blankets and take their ease. They were now in a high, flat country, where trees were scarce and the brush all spiky with thorns and new leaves.

Four years ago he had come up this road to North Texas. It was a year after Maria Luisa died. He had moved out of that graceful Spanish town of San Antonio with its two-story stone buildings and the ornate cast-iron balconies, their cottage roofs shingled with slate. The old Spanish houses all had their backs to the river. The owners of those homes carefully kept record of their descent from the original settlers from the Canary Islands who had come in 1733, the Betancorts, the Reales, they had retreated behind polished wooden window bars. They retreated into the cool of tiled floors. Into the gestures of fans and mantillas and morning mass at San Fernando, increasingly hemmed in by German Catholics and Irish Catholics in the pews, people with incomprehensible languages. Spain, Daughter of Light, Defender of the Faith, Hammer of the Moors, sadly faded.

He recalled excursions on the river, the girls so like their mother with gray eyes and dark curling hair and boats passing by offering melons. The immense cypresses. The one that was a hundred feet tall knee deep in the San Antonio River. Joyous memories.

When he met her he had been setting up his own print shop on Plaza de Armas, slinging ink and type, deeply engaged in the process of making words appear on paper. He could pick up a stick of type and read it backward, he knew from the sound of the paten if it would be a good print or not. He knew his inks and his papers. He delighted in these perfectly printed messages to the world even if he were not carrying them personally.

What good was a beautiful town like that when she was not there? He turned his face to the sky in an effort to clear his head. They went away and never said another word to you again. In some strange way it made him mad. Not a word, not a sign. No messages from the Other World, or perhaps there were signs and he did not see them. He watched two caracara eagles sailing on their black pirate wings, their red hoods and white vests, and heard Johanna singing "Hard Times": *Iss the song and the sigh of the willy* . . .

Weary, he corrected her, smiling.

Yes Kep-dun, is willy, sigh of a willy.

They were only a few miles from Lampasas now; around them the creosote bushes were stiff as bones. Their rounded leaves vibrated in the wind. To the north streams of cirrus were like a frosted sandstorm, veils of high-borne mist poured out of the Polar regions. Perhaps more storms to come.

Soon they would come to the hill country. It was scored by deep canyons and high bluffs. Clear streams cut through layers of limestone. There would be more cover there for raiding parties of Kiowa and Comanche but they would deal with that when they came to it. They pressed on. The wheels of the excursion wagon lifted a spume of dust in yellow and pink. For a long time he could see no other wagons but themselves.

But after a while they came upon an elderly lady in a gig. He could see it from a long way off as a jiggling dark roundish thing like a beetle that resolved itself into a vehicle with the quavering legs of a long bony horse pulling it. An accordion top rose over the two wheels.

Well, here is somebody, she said. She pulled up beside them. She was trim and small and wore a new-fashioned pancake hat in straw tipped rakishly to one side. Her white hair was done up in a roll all around the bottom of her head and she wore tight brown driving gloves.

Yes ma'am, and where are you going?

I am going all the way to Durand. I believe I can make it in three days. People have tried to discourage me from this journey but I ignore them. I have a lawsuit to pursue.

I see, said the Captain. From . . . ?

Lampasas.

Then you will do me a favor, please. He reached down for his canvas bag of coins. I would be obliged if you would take these two fifty-cent pieces to the fellow at the stave mill there in Durand. The one that makes the brooms.

That animal, she said. Whatever you are paying him for he doesn't deserve it. I have half a mind to refuse.

I wish you wouldn't. We inadvertently came away with two of his hens and I would not be known as a chicken thief. It has been bothering me.

There is no chicken in Texas worth half a dollar in silver, sir.

I consider it an apology, of a sort.

You have a tender conscience.

Chicken thieves are not highly regarded.

True. Give it here, then.

He stepped down and brought the coins over to her. Many thanks, he said. He lifted his sweat-stained old field hat.

And where are you going?

To Castroville, the Captain said. I'm a seed buyer.

Very well. That girl has a peculiar stare. Is she disturbed in her mind in some way?

The Captain got back into the wagon and picked up the reins from the driver's post. No, he said. I wish you a safe journey.

AT NOON HE put the saddle on Pasha. He would ride alongside the packhorse's head. This was not friendly country. As he put the saddle on he finally gave in to old age and reached for one of the sheep fleeces out of their stack of blankets and threw it across the saddle seat. So much more comfortable than the hard leather. Johanna watched, her dark blue eyes mild and

understanding now that the strange old woman was gone. He
snapped a lead on a ring of Fancy's driving bridle and held the
lead in one hand as they went on. Their water bottles were full.
It would do. They would be at Lampasas soon. Pasha's easy
smooth walk was a joy to ride and the Captain could not help
but pat his neck and fool with his mane and try to get it to lie all
on one side.

THERE WAS QUITE a lot of trouble in Lampasas. He knew this
from when he had passed through years earlier. It was one of
those feuds between two families, each with a large number of
sons. It seemed to be one of the rules or laws of human nature.
The boys all grow up together and then they become young men
and they fight, at first in play, and then somebody gets hurt, and
before you know it the revenge drama is on.

Around them the dun-colored pelt of grasses shone in the
thin sunlight as if it were studded with mica and quartz and
now with the days growing longer the first green shoots grew up
beneath. He began to see more people on the road going toward
Lampasas. As best he could calculate it was a Saturday and perhaps the people in this region found it their custom to come to
town to shop or celebrate or seek out company on a Saturday
and stay all night to sleep off a hangover or go to church in the
morning or both.

It was now the second week in March and a time of tender
growth, when it slowly dawned on people that the world would
not always be cold and brown. This high level country was like
something unexpectedly and suddenly loved and respond-
ing to the bounty of young rain and longer hours of sunlight.

Awake, awake, ye drowsy sleeper. The wind was fresh and
wet. They drove through the Brooke crossing of the Lampasas
River. As in all semi-arid regions the green was all in the river-
beds, the ravines, the stream crossings where water gathered
and the wind sailed overhead. Thick colonies of Carrizo cane
grew in the little valley of the Lampasas and they shook their
glossy plumes in concert.

When they reached the level again, the Captain and Johanna
came across a group of four men on horseback, with stampede
strings hanging down their backs and hair-tassels at the end of
the strings. They were all armed. They pulled up their horses
strung straight across the road. They were the people now being called "cowboys," an occupational specialty that moved
into place as the buffalo were shot in their millions.

He pulled up Pasha and Fancy. Johanna would be troubled
and so he got down and came to stand beside her where she sat
on the front seat. After a moment's stillness she stood up and
vaulted over the backrest with her skirts flying and dropped
down in the wagon bed between the water butt and the box of
food and cooking supplies. She took to the *jorongo* as an otter
slides into his hole.

Curative Waters, said one of the men.

Bullet holes, said another.

They wore broad-brimmed hats against the relentless sun,
the brims shading the V of skin showing in their open shirt collars. They carried reatas at the right-hand side of their saddles.
All of them right-handed. They were riding Mother Hubbard
saddles with big flat horns and a flank cinch. Bunches of piggin'
strings tied on the left side.

Where y'all coming from?

Durand, the Captain said. And we are headed to Castroville, fifteen miles west of San Antonio. Would you like me to get out a map and show you?

No sir, said another. I know where it is. Shooter Weiss gets seed from there. He paused. I don't know how to spell his name. He's a Kraut.

Then it would be S-c-h-u-t-e-r, said the Captain. Now, is there any particular reason you are blocking my road?

They turned to one another and their horses shifted. They were small horses with thick, long manes and tails that swept the road. Mustangs. The horses had sloped back ends like whippets.

There's been a lot of raiding between here and Castroville, said one. The Comanches and the Kiowa are driving people out of the hill country. They got cover down there. Can't see them coming, like up here. It's almost empty down there. People driven out. You had best take care.

I will.

Well, are you going into Lampasas?

That's where this road goes. And since it is apparently the only one, I did not contemplate riding straight off into the trackless wilds of Lampasas County. Is there some other road you could recommend?

The tallest one among them said, Sir, I remember you from when you read your newspapers there one time in Meridian. I was most interested to hear all the news. So I tell you what. You might not want to go into Wiley and Toland's saloon, it's called The Gem. I am telling you because you ought to know that the

Horrell brothers find refreshment there when they are not out shooting down Mexican persons.

You don't say. And they would object to my appearing there?

They all looked at one another.

Tell him, said one.

Well then, the tallest one said. They are all wrapped around the axle about the Eastern newspapers, the ones that show engravings of cowboys, and they think they ought to be appearing in them. And if you show up to read the news they are going to start hassling you to read about *them*.

You are joking.

I am not. They are mentally not very fast. They are every one of them one brick short of a load. And when we heard of you coming I said, Well, by God—excuse me young lady—(he touched his hat)—that there must be the Captain come to read his newspapers. And so, me and my brothers, we heard you read in Meridian one time and we were impressed by all the happenings everywhere and everything, and we sure liked your reading.

The others nodded. Johanna saw the man touch his hat and look at her and wondered what it meant. Perhaps a warning. He might throw it at her, he might be directing a curse of some sort at her.

You are very kind, said the Captain.

And I said, I bet the Horrell brothers is going to expect themselves to be in the Eastern newspapers and when they are not they are going to raise Old Jack with the Captain. And besides there's going to be some kind of a meeting about a farmer's union and a dance and they get all excited. Benjamin starts in stuttering.

That's thinking ahead, said one of the others. He turned, loose and supple at the waist, to keep the Captain in view as his restive little horse spun to the left in a quick move to unseat him. He kept it going right on around and brought it back to where it had been in the first place, facing the Captain and said, Quit that you son of a bitch. He touched his hat. Excuse me young lady.

Johanna sat with a stilled face inside the *jorongo,* her favorite cave of red wool, her magical protection.

I appreciate your concern, the Captain said.

Happy to be of service, said the tall one. We are busting cattle out of the brush over there on Bean Creek and we come across old Mrs. Becker going north on the Durand road and she said she seen you and you was worried about some stolen chickens. So we came riding back to find you.

Ah well, a minor matter, said the Captain. He stood beside Pasha and patted his jaw, sat his hat lower on his forehead.

Yes sir. So my brother here said, Well, that's Captain Kidd and we'd best leave our work and go warn him. Those cows can stay laid up one more day. They ain't going to get no wilder than they already are.

Another brother said, Not possible.

A third said, We'll be around here somewhere, you know, for the night.

Kidd nodded slowly. You have no bedrolls, he said.

Yes sir, well, we just lay down on the ground and sleep.

I see. The Captain was silent a moment, puzzling over the Horrell brothers, people whose minds were lost in such delusions, such avid desire for worldly fame.

And what about the English newspapers? said the Captain. Do they expect themselves to be on the front page of the London *Times*?

Sir, said the taller one. The Horrells don't know there *is* a England.

Well. Thank you so much for this excellent information. The Captain stepped into the stirrup and was proud of the fact that at age seventy-one he could step up from the ground onto a sixteen-hand horse. With some pain but no flinching he swung into the saddle. Clearly there was no question of doing a reading at all. He said, I will be sure to park my traps and gear and this delicate young lady nearby the springs and never stir until I can get the hell out of Lampasas.

No, seventy-two. He had just turned seventy-two on March 15, yesterday, as he had turned sixteen just before Horseshoe Bend and at that time it would have been beyond belief that he would even live to see this age, much less be traveling along a distant road far to the west, still in one piece, alive and unaccountably happy.

SEVENTEEN

———◆———

H E HAD DECIDED to avoid the Horrell brothers at all costs, but the Horrell brothers found them.

The Captain was unlimbering where they had parked beside the beautiful Lampasas springs and the giant live oaks that surrounded them. The spring was in a low place, one of the soothing green low places of this high and dry country, and made a reflective pond. The surface tossed glittering reflections against the trunks. On one side was a stand of Carrizo cane, graceful and green. It had tall plumed heads. Great limbs overhead were alive with birds on their spring migration to the north, lately come up from Mexico; the quick and nervous robins, the low song of a yellow oriole, painted buntings in their outrageous clown colors.

The Horrell brothers sat on their horses and watched as the Captain and Johanna began unloading their gear. They rode good horses, Copperbottom breeds, Steel Dust lineage. The Captain could see it in the lines of their bodies. They sat and watched Pasha narrowly as he grazed in the long grasses at the verge of the spring. The live oaks were high overhead and the evening breeze moved over the surface of the water. The Captain ignored them.

You're the man that reads the news.

Yes, I am.

Well how come we ain't in the news?

I don't know, the Captain said. I don't write the newspapers.

I'm Merritt Horrell and this is Tom and he's my brother, and these are my other brothers here. Mart and Benjamin and Sam.

The five brothers wore various articles of dress that had been pieced together out of military uniforms from both sides, missing buttons and faded to an unvarying slate color. One had two different kinds of stirrups, one metal, one wood, and none of their hats seemed to fit. The youngest, or at least the smallest, no more than fourteen by the look of him, wore a derby far too big for his head and the Captain realized the boy had stuffed the inside band with rags or paper to make it fit. It seemed suspended over his small head. Whatever woman had raised these five boys must now be in the county asylum, if Lampasas County had one, and if they did not, they had best build one soon.

Enchanted, gentlemen, he said. Maybe you *are* in the news. You could well be in the news back in the east. Say, Chicago or the little one-sheet paper in Ball Ground, Georgia. Just think. The Captain shook out his newspapers. Perhaps London or even California.

Well, we should be, said Merritt. He had a dull stare that was also strangely intent. We killed a right smart of Mexicans. You'd think they'd put in something.

He took off his hat and slapped the edge of his hand into the crown to straighten the crease. He looked as if he had combed his stiff yellow hair with a skillet.

Kidd nodded and said, And nobody objects to your killing a right smart of Mexicans?

Ain't nobody. Merritt replaced his hat and then crossed his hands on the saddle horn. Governor Davis chucked out everbody that was with the Confederacy and never replaced them. Some Army people come around sometimes. I guess they would object probably.

Could be. The Captain reached for a roll of rope and turned and strung it between two trees and began to throw the blankets over it to air them.

Would they be doing a wood engraving of us?

I have no idea.

He looked up and saw Johanna on the far side of the spring, watching from the Carrizo cane. This surprised him. She could move so silently when she wanted. She was an apparition of flying hair and bare feet in the deepening shadows. The cane plumes rose and fell with the chilly breeze, all around and above her head.

Well, said Merritt. Come to the saloon in town, it's called The Gem, the other one is The Great Western, but come to The Gem and read your news. Telling how we pursued the hated Red Man and everthing, how the Higgins brothers cruelly murdered, et cetera. Despite Davis's pitiless state police and like that.

I hope you won't mind if I am late.

No sir, not at all. You come anytime. If people don't want to hear you read about us, well then, we would not object to them leaving.

And so he did not go, but sat up and waited and before nine o'clock by his hunting watch he could tell from the noise in town the Horrells were probably drunk. He could hear them all the way from the springs; sounds of music and shouts, far away and thin. He watched the night world and heard its sounds. He smelled tobacco smoke. He watched Pasha; the horse lifted his head from his grazing and stared across the spring at what Kidd guessed were other horses but did not call out. The Captain saw the glow of a cigarette. The Merritt brothers were there and guarding him and Johanna as they said they would. They would take turns, watch on watch. He did not sleep at all that night but sat leaning against a wheel with his revolver in hand and they left before it was daylight.

EIGHTEEN

———•◆•———

THEY CAME SOUTH into the hill country at last. And here everything was still.

He rode Pasha and put a sort of blanket saddle pad on the packhorse under the harness and the butcher knife in his waistband as well as his revolver. If the raiders came he would cut the packhorse out of the harness and throw Johanna on the saddle pad and they would run for it and abandon the wagon. Perhaps looting the wagon would slow them down.

The Comanches mostly came from the north, down from the Red River, across the open arid country around Lampasas. The dust they raised could be seen for miles and so they skirted the towns and forts. When they came on south to the hill country there was concealment and water and isolated farms. They loved the hill country with a raider's passion. Here was fighting and here was loot with no soldiers to stop them.

The world fell away from beneath the wheels of the *Curative Waters* wagon, valley after valley, ridge after ridge falling away to the blue horizon.

As they came to the top of a rise he kept carefully to one side of the road so they could not be skylighted and stopped. He would sit for fifteen, twenty minutes at a time looking and listening for signs of life, for raiding parties. He listened for the quarreling bark of a squirrel, disturbed by riders. He watched the buzzards circling overhead, looking for both the tight spiral that meant a dead body somewhere, a carcass either human or animal, and also for their sudden dips, for they were curious birds and would drop like stones on those remarkable wings to inspect something new or unusual.

Johanna watched as well. She did not play with her cat's cradles or make up sentences in English. She wore the confining shoes and laid the shotgun longways at her feet. He did not smoke his pipe. The distinctive odor carried for long distances. And also he took in the air for the scent of others' tobacco smoke. Nothing. The wind had dropped. From the rises he inspected the tops of the trees below, both before and behind the rise, the live oak and the bur oak, the occasional hickories in ravines, for movement that was not made by the wind. Nothing. So they went on.

He kept the packhorse's lead in his hand. They started in the early morning when the stars told their way from east to west. They passed abandoned farms, little cabins with stone fencing here and there. Some had been burned down.

They came through the red granite country north of Llano. Mountains of red and pink granite. The valleys were starred with Mexican hat and gayfeather waving in tall magenta rods, bluebonnets by the acre. It was flowering time in the hill country. New grass for their horses, tender growth for the whitetail deer, and at night a ringtail cat with it sixteen-stripe tail and bat ears and eyes big as buckeyes carefully raised a kernel of corn from the horse's spillage, lifted the kernel to its cat mouth while they silently watched. It sat curious and fearless at the farthest edge of the firelight while Johanna whispered to it in Kiowa, inflections of delight.

They came to a destroyed cabin and he pulled up and then went inside. Broken cups and pieces of dress material torn on a nail. A doll's body without a head. He dug a .50-caliber bullet out of the wall with his knife and then carefully placed it on the windowsill as if for a memento. Here were memories, loves, deep heartstring notes like the place where he had been raised in Georgia. Here had been people whose dearest memories were the sound of a dipper dropped in the water bucket after taking a drink and the click of it as it hit bottom. The quiet of evening. The shade of the Devil's trumpet vine over a window, scattered shadows gently hypnotic. The smell of a new calf, a long bar of sun falling into the back door over worn planks and every knot outlined. The familiar path to the barn walked for years by one's father, grandfather, uncles, the way they called out, *Horses, horses.* How they swung the bucket by the handle as they went at an easy walk down the path between the trees, between here and there, between babyhood and adulthood, between innocence and death, that worn path and the lifting of the heart as the horses called out to you, how you knew each by the sound of its voice in the long cool evening after a day of hard work. Your heart melted sweetly, it slowed, lost its edges. *Horses, horses.* All gone in the burning.

Once at evening they came downhill to a stream crossing where the clear water made its way between great curving bluffs.

Level strata of limestone in stripe after stripe carved back into a deep hollow with the big trees hanging down from overhead. It was like being in a tunnel. Maidenhair fern in bright lime-colored bouquets grew out of the limestone where water seeped through and it smelled of water and wet stone and the green fern. There was a small springhouse made of logs backed into the hollow. He looked into it; little troughs carved in the stone for milk jugs, a square pool for cheeses and perhaps for meat in metal containers. The water was cold.

There were deep holes of water here, quite clear. A big one just downstream of the crossing. From a distance they heard somebody shouting, over the hilltops or from a hilltop. In what language he could not tell. He stood still for a long time and listened. Then the shouting stopped. He and the girl sat in silence for a long time but it did not begin again.

Nevertheless, she needed a swim and a bath with the soap and so he backed the *Curative Waters* wagon into a very small valley that led into the larger stream. He unhitched Fancy and filled the horse's morales with hard corn. He led them far up the narrowing little valley and its thick foliage and tied them and waited until they had eaten and then left them there, hidden. That would keep them safe for the night although they would be hard to handle in the morning after being tied up all night. But he could not take a chance on losing them by letting them free to graze.

He came back to the running stream and sat with his back turned while Johanna jumped into the deep pool and swam in her Bad Water Lady of Durand drawers and shift, silently, carefully. No splashing. Soap bubbles drifted noiselessly down the stream. He washed his face in a basin and shaved and at supper, cooked over a small fire quickly doused, they sat eating and listening. Raiding parties of young men had their own laws and their own universe in which the niceties of civilized warfare did not count and an old man and a young girl were fair game to them, for in the Indian Wars there were no civilians. After a while the Captain and Johanna went to sit in the springhouse and listen to the soft clatter of running water. In the shadows they could keep watch and perhaps sleep a little. The running water was soothing and sweet.

Two great live oaks overhung the stream from above. They dropped their leaves one at a time into the water. The new leaves were coming in and pushing off the old ones slowly, slowly. They were small and hard. They fell like pennies.

And looking out of the springhouse window he saw one of the great drooping limbs overhead begin to shake. Its farthing leaves came down in a light shower.

He drew in his breath in a small sound. He thought at first the enormous live oak was at last coming loose from its tenuous hold on the bank overhead and would fall. He had seen it happen once before. The girl woke up and came to stand beside him in the shadow and look through the minute window.

Out of the broad limbs a figure dropped. It was so startling that it seemed to take forever. A slim young man with long blond hair fell and fell. He held his bow and quiver overhead with one hand. The moon shone on him as he fell. His hair flowed up over his head like spun flax, a cloud of gold. It was cut short on one side—Kiowa. He struck the water and thin fans like crystal erupted around him.

He then surfaced and skimmed through the water to the bank. He held his weapons over his head.

Captain Kidd turned his hand with the revolver in it so that the barrel pointed out. The water reflections made deep blue planes under his eyes. He wondered if she would betray him. If she would call out to the young captive and his fellows who hid above on the bluff somewhere. If this was his last night on earth. This was what she had wanted so much, to return to the Kiowa and the life she had known. The people whom she considered her people, and their gods her gods.

But when he turned and looked into her eyes she put her hand on his arm. She shook her head once. Then they saw three others drop out of the live oak, one after the other, flinging great screens of water around themselves as they broke the surface and swam to the bank. Soft noises of Kiowa. Quiet murmurs. And then they slipped away.

Perhaps they both had narrowly escaped death—death by arrow, death by beauty, death by night.

AND SO THEY went on south to Castroville.

They came through Fredericksburg, a small town in the hill country, beleaguered, nervous, inept at defense. The population was almost entirely German. He had heard it called Fritztown. The main street going through town was wide enough for three or four vehicles to pass abreast and was an open invitation for warriors to gallop straight down the middle and fire in both directions if they wished.

Slowly and soundlessly the evening sun poured its red light down the main street. The lights of the hotel came on, dust bloomed up at Fancy's heels. The Captain took two rooms as usual and paid for baths and a washerwoman. The people came around the green excursion wagon to stare when they heard the Captain and Johanna's names from the hotel owner. The girl was Johanna Leonberger, a captive who had been redeemed for German coin silver. They had heard about the silver from the grandfather of Bianca Babb who had brought his granddaughter back from Indian Territory.

They gave him advice and warnings; of how the captives were strange, how they disliked white people, how they had peculiar eyes and had probably partaken of some secret potion or drug to make them so. That was the only answer, the only reasonable explanation.

The Captain offered to do a reading even though he knew very few people would come because so few people here were conversant with English and especially newspaper English. Or where things were in the outside world. It was in the main to help Johanna learn the proper protocol for sitting at the door and collecting dimes. And in reality, the fewer people to attend, the better. It was a practice session. He put up his advertisements and was given the use of the Vereins Kirche for that night. He asked for a blacksmith to fix his broken tire but the local blacksmith had been killed on the road to Kerrville.

In her room they shared a supper of some German dish made of noodles and ground mutton and a cream sauce. He still could not trust her manners in a restaurant. But she carefully placed her napkin on her knee and lifted each bite on her fork straight up to the level of her mouth and then aimed it straight in.

Is all lite Cho-henna?

I suppose that will do, he said.

She slurped a noodle until it flipped up and struck her on the nose.

Johanna!

She laughed until tears came to her eyes. She wiped her hair out of her face and addressed herself once again to the food. The Captain tried to be stern and then gave up. He set to the dish and the preserved cauliflower to one side with enthusiasm. It had been a long time since he had eaten a well-cooked supper or anything made with milk or cream and they did not have to wash up the dishes in a bucket.

That watch, she said. He took it out of his pocket and opened it.

In thirty minutes, he said, holding it out. We must go read at seven.

It is when the little hand there on seven and big hand on that twelve?

That's it, my dear, he said. Then he pointed down the hall to the bathroom and handed her a towel. Go, he said.

AT THE VEREINS Kirche, the People's Church, which was both a church and a community hall and a fort if need be, he sat her down at the door with the paint can on a fern stand beside her.

Dime-ah, he said. He held up his hand. Sit. Stay. Then he walked out the door, turned, and walked back in and pretended to notice Johanna for the first time, and said, Ten cents?

She understood instantly and pointed to the paint can. Dime-ah! She said it sternly and with great firmness. And so that evening he read from several Eastern papers while Johanna took up the task of being gatekeeper as if she had been waiting for something like this all her life. She fixed every person who came in with her glassy blue stare and pointed to the can and said, Dime-ah, tin sintz, a small girl with bottom teeth like a white fence and braided ochre hair and a dress in carriage check. From somewhere she had dredged up yet another word in German and when someone walked past without noticing her she cried out, *Achtung!* Tin sintz!

Joy and liveliness had come back to his readings now. His voice had its old vibrancy again and he smiled as he read the amusing things, the Hindi women who would not say their husband's names, odd telegraph messages caught by a reporter, and recalled how dull his life had seemed before he had come upon her in Wichita Falls. He saw her bright, fierce little face break into laughter when the crowd laughed. It was good. Laughter is good for the soul and all your interior works.

THAT NIGHT HE walked back to the hotel with her and put her to bed in her own room. She yawned enormously and said, Big hoas liddle hoas, wiped her hands on the bedcover, yawned again. Then she fell back on the bed and was asleep within moments. He tiptoed out. He knew that by the morning she would be sleeping on the floor. But still this was an improvement. Their washed and ironed clothes lay in a bundle at his door so that they could be clean and civilized by morning. He thought about how Johanna was being filed down and her sharp edges ground away. The Captain sat by his lamp and tried to find articles in his newspapers that were not tied to dates; fluff pieces on chemical discoveries and astronomical surprises. Alphonse Borrelly had discovered an asteroid and named it Lydia and the

Earl of Rosse had calculated the surface temperature of the moon at 500 degrees Fahrenheit. That would do in a pinch. He laid out his traveling clothes, the old rough flannel plaid Plains shirt, his lace-ups, his clean socks. It was forty miles of rough country south to Bandera and were they to be killed and scalped their bodies would be found bloody but spruce.

He broke down the .38, cleaned it, reassembled it. He made a list: feed, flour, ammunition, soap, beef, candles, faith, hope, charity.

NINETEEN

———•———

Finally they came into the town of Bandera where Polish immigrants labored at a saw mill and lines of freight wagons and their oxen stood in the street to make up a convoy to San Antonio as protection against the Comanche. The great oxen came in teams of six and eight down the main street with their heads tipping from one side to the other with every stride as if they were listening to some unheard music, a ponderous waltz. The people still believed the red men came only on the full moon, despite all evidence to the contrary, and the moon was now well past full and so the people in Bandera lived in delusions of safety.

In Bandera he found that the blacksmith was overwhelmed with work for the freighters, shoeing the teams of oxen and repairing tie-rods and beating out carriage bolts on the anvil. So he let it go; it seemed the cracked iron rim would have to hold a little longer.

The Captain rented the Davenport Mercantile building and for an hour's reading they made enough to get through the final miles to Castroville. He had mined his newspapers for the last bits of news. Texas finally readmitted to the Union, for instance.

He adjusted his reading glasses in the light of the bull's-eye. Cincinnati Red Stockings, the first professional baseball team, a new concept in sport . . . Ada Kepley, first female law college graduate . . . construction of the new bridge from Manhattan to Brooklyn continuing . . . a donkey adopted as the symbol of the Democrat party . . . the Vaudeville Theatre opened on The Strand in London, shocking exposure of female limbs on stage. By this time Johanna had lost her fear of crowds of white people and so she sat at the door and held out the paint can for the admittance fee. The Captain knew she regarded the coins as ammunition as much as a medium of exchange. Her head moved in birdlike jerks from face to face and if anyone tried to get past without paying she seized a sleeve in her small, hard hand and cried, Dime-ah! Chohenna choot!

They did not understand her but the meaning was clear.

THE HILLS FELL away behind them until they were nothing more than an uneven blue line on the horizon. There were no gradual approaches in or out of the hill country. They came down from the hills and then they were in the short-grass prairie in one geological moment. They had descended to a lower altitude and thus the breeze at evening carried the soft breath of the Gulf of Mexico and the lower Rio Grande and the smell of mesquite and the palms of Resaca de la Palma and even the smoke of the cannon those long years ago, almost thirty years. It would stay with him always as everything you ever did stayed with you, every horse you ever saddled, every morning he awoke with Maria Luisa beside him, and every slap of the paten on fresh paper, every time he had thrown open the shutters in the Betancort house, and his captain dying under his hands, always there like a tangle of telegraph wires in the brain where no dispatch was ever lost, what an odd thing, an odd thing. The soft breeze out of the south with its hint of salt lifted Fancy's mane.

Kep-dun?

Yes, Johanna?

Mine doll.

He thought for a moment. He said, The doll you left up on the Red River.

Yes, mine doll, she looking across. Looking, looking. The girl opened her hands on her lap. You read now Castroville? I say dime-ah, tin sintz?

No, Johanna. Not anymore. The Captain's heart seemed to be shaky and somewhat erratic. Not anymore, my dear.

She sat close to him on the driver's seat and put her hand in the crook of his arm. Yes, she said.

No. He pointed ahead. *Onkle*, he said. *Tante*.

She felt the arrival of something chilling, something wrong. Something lonely. He was the only person she had left in the world and the only human being she now knew. He was strong and wise and they had fought together at the springs. She ate with a fork now and wore the horrible dresses without complaint. What had she done wrong? Something was wrong. They drove through a cheerless flat landscape of mesquite and brush and the occasional fields. White people passed them in wagons. The break in the iron tire made a sound like an infinitely slow clock: click, click click.

Kontah laff! she cried out. Ha! Ha! Ha! He turned and saw tears running down her small face and the freckles stood out brightly in sweat and heat. She drew up her checkered skirts and wiped her face. *Kontah?*

You'll adjust, he said in a firm voice. I have accepted a good round fee as well as given a promise to return you to your relatives. I am a man of my word.

Kontah klepp honts! She tried to smile.

And to do otherwise would be dishonorable and it would be robbery. No, I am not going to klepp my honts.

Her head dropped now until her taffy-colored hair fell in a curtain over her hot face. She understood his tone of voice and the stiffness of his arm. Somewhere ahead were strange white people she could only remember as if in poorly lit lantern slides called aunt and uncle and that they were going to them. The rest she could figure out for herself but not why, or where *Kontah* would go. The wind brought no news of her people. They were gone forever. She drew her hand away from his arm and her skirt hems rolled in the breeze. Still she wept. The broken tire rim counted out the hours and miles, click click click.

They left the north-south road from the hill country to the San Antonio road and turned off to the west. They drove through a country now being sliced up by plows. Those plowing in the fields turned to look at the *Curative Waters* wagon and stared after them as they passed.

Castroville was a collection of stone houses with high-pitched roofs, some big square two-story ones with gallerias all around the second story, long windows, the women shaking out dust cloths and rugs from the balconies and powdering the heads of people on the street. It looked like all the engravings that the Captain had seen of European villages except for the cactus and the mesquite growing in yards. In their custom they lived in villages and then went out every day to work in their fields. The Captain had shed his canvas coat on the first day of April and now drove in gartered shirtsleeves and galluses. Down here in the flat land it was very warm and any wind was welcome. At least he had brought them through alive, the horses in good condition.

They passed the inn and gristmill where it sat on the Medina River among wild pecan trees. A seminary of the Order of Mary Immaculate took up an entire three acres and in every street abided the careful and precise pacing of life as it was lived in Alsace-Lorraine. The big warehouse of the Huth Seed Company was cavernous and dim with shade. Pasha tied behind called out to other horses but finally gave it up because there were now so many.

Captain Kidd was told that Wilhelm and Anna Leonberger lived fifteen miles farther on to the west, in a daughter community called D'Hanis. That the graves of the Leonberger couple and their little daughter were at St. Dominic's church there. He did not tell anyone of Johanna's captivity or her parents. They would come in crowds. They would come bearing cakes and pies and featherbeds. The little boys would whistle and the girls stare at her expressionless face and the adults would speak to her in the Alsatian dialect. As they drove on west beyond Castroville, on the dusty caliche road, the towering steeple and the roof of St. Dominic's rose from the level horizon.

They stood before the graves. The Captain took off his hat and put it over his breast as he had been taught to do so long ago, the proper behavior. The girl looked at the headstones and their weeping angels with some curiosity, mostly indifference, and then turned to look all around herself at a country tamed and torn with plows and weighted down with stone buildings.

We go back Dallas? she said. I don't like here. She was composed and quiet and she would try one last time. I don't like here, pliss Kep-dun, pliss.

We can't, my dear. He stepped into the driver's seat and took up the reins. We just cannot.

Still she stood by the grave and then lifted her head to the flat countryside. A woodenness came over her. A Kiowa's first and last resort was courage. A Kiowa did not beg or plead or appease. She knew at the bitter end she could starve away the despair, deny any sustenance to surrender. She wiped her face again and climbed up into the wagon. *Ausay gya kii, gyao boi tol.* Prepare for a hard winter, prepare for hard times. She braided her hair as if for battle. And so she became quiet and stilled.

They rode on in silence, through the bright, dry landscape and through the hot afternoon hours, click click click.

The Captain stopped a man on horseback.

He said, Sir, I would be grateful if you would do me a favor. I would be willing to pay you whatever you ask.

And what would that be?

The man sat his horse easily as it turned and twisted. The man wore a white shirt and dark vest with his wool suit coat tied behind the saddle. He regarded the Captain, a distinguished-looking man, clearly an *Amerikaner*, in a wagon with gold lettering and bullet holes.

The Captain said, Give me directions to Wilhelm and Anna Leonberger's farm and then ride on ahead of me and give them the message that Johanna Leonberger, who is the daughter of Jan and Greta, missing these four years, is come from captivity among the Kiowas.

For a moment the man stared at him and then at Johanna. She looked back at him with eyes blue and hard as delft.

Then he cried out, God be praised!

The man shouted this out to the sky and without another word he turned his horse and went galloping away down the road and the last the Captain saw of him he had turned south, beyond St. Dominic's. Springtime birds shot up out of the tall grass and to his right lay that long blue serrated line of the hills they had just left, distant and somehow safe.

THEY CAME DOWN a long straight road that led to the Leonberger farm. He got down first and held out his hand to Johanna. The girl had become blank again, blank as bone. Without moving her head she turned her eyes to look at her relatives' farm. The stone house with its long front porch running the length of the building, the sort of porch Texans called a galleria, a paling fence, chickens, farm tools, a barn, mesquite trees, dogs, the blazing sun. The man the Captain had sent ahead stood smiling and holding his horse's reins. He was staring at Johanna. Nobody said anything. Dogs came to surround them and terrify them with barking.

Raus! Raus! A man came out and beat the dogs off with a riding quirt. Johanna's head snapped up at the sound of the German language and then, as if they had just appeared, looked from right to left at the farmhouse and the outbuildings and the broad sweep of the south brush country with the mesquite beaten back to the field edges and the flowering huisache, the tall candelabra of yucca blooms, thick and fleshy and white. *Tante*, she whispered. *Onkle.*

Captain Kidd took off his hat. He said, I am Jefferson Kyle Kidd, and I have returned your niece, Johanna. She was ransomed by Indian Agent Samuel Hammond at Fort Sill, Indian Territory.

He handed over the papers and stood in silence as if in a winter blizzard. His throat hurt. He was tired. His eyebrow hurt and the sharp pains had begun to creep around on his skull. His hands looked as bony and wrinkled as those of a catacomb mummy. Johanna crossed the driver's seat to drop down beside him on the ground.

Anna Leonberger came out to stand beside her husband. Captain Kidd waited for another interminable few seconds while the man read the papers. The Captain said, finally, I have brought her all the way from Wichita Falls on the Red River.

Ja, yes, is what Adolph says. Wilhelm Leonberger motioned with one hand toward the messenger without looking up. He was still making his way through the paper. He was a slight blond man with a tanned face in brown planes. He turned to look at Adolph and then back to the Captain. He said, We send up fifty dollar in gold.

Yes, said Captain Kidd. I bought this wagon with it.

Wilhelm looked at it and the gold lettering, *Curative Waters,* and the bullet holes. He said, And the harness too?

Yes.

You have receipt?

No, said Captain Kidd. I do not.

Wilhelm regarded Johanna. She stood with one hand on Fancy's harness, barefooted, her shoes tied around her neck, and she was gripping the back band so tightly her knuckles were white. Her hair was braided up and around her head. Her dress skirts in madder and yellow carriage check lifted and fell in the flatland wind.

Wilhelm said, Her parents were done murder by the Indians.

I heard that, said the Captain. Yes. A tragedy.

The man who had served as messenger had an anxious look on his face. He said something loud and cheerful in Alsatian and then lifted his shoulders to the Captain. *We are not all like this,* the shrug said.

All right, vell then, come in, I suppose.

The messenger bit his lip in dismay and hesitated and then mounted and rode away.

TWENTY

———•◆•———

I<small>T DID NOT</small> matter what the Captain said to Wilhelm Leonberger, that the girl needed quiet and peace and a gradual adjustment to her new circumstances, that she thought of herself as a Kiowa and must slowly be brought to learn European behavior all over again, that she had changed guardians three times now and needed reassurance. He knew that the news was too good, too electrifying to keep to oneself. Soon they would come, probably with the priest, they would come with songs and praise and thankfulness and sausages and cakes *mit schlage über*. They would cry out words in German to her, to see if she remembered. They would hold out to her tintypes of her parents, a dress she had had when she was six. *Remember? Remember?*

The Captain sat on a horsehair sofa with a cup of strong coffee in one hand and a seed cake in the other. Johanna had fallen into a corner on her haunches with her hands clasped around her ankles and her skirts bunched up in her elbows, staring at all the things the white people collected and put inside their immovable houses. The daguerreotypes, which to her were strange metal plates with odd arrangements of blacks and whites. The doilies, the carpet with violently orange and garnet flowers, glass in the windows and ironstone dishes standing up on a sideboard like plate armor, fragile little side tables. There were drapes hanging in front of the windows against all logic. She did not know why one would make windows in a stone wall and put glass in them and then cover them over with cloth.

Get up, the woman said. Get up now.

Johanna regarded her with a serious and searching gaze and then turned away.

We found them with the brains out, said Wilhelm. My brother and his wife. The savages spill out the brains and then stuff in the grass. In the skull. Like hen nest.

I see, said the Captain. His coffee was growing cold. With some determination, he drank it.

Her mother they outrage.

Terrible, said Captain Kidd.

Then kill in pieces.

Unspeakable. He shook his head. His stomach felt suddenly unstable.

Anna was a thin woman, defined and accurate in her gestures. She was dark with the smooth olive skin and black eyes of Bavarians. She turned her head slowly, slowly, and looked at the girl defiantly sitting on the floor in a welter of madder-and-yellow-checked skirts, the lace edging torn off, hard bare feet, her hair spraying out of its braids, and then pressed her lips into a tight line and regarded her shoe toes.

Anna said, The little sister they kill by the troat being cut. They hang her by a leg on the big tree on the Sabinal where is the store there. Anna shut her hands together. No chasing will catch them. The men all chased. They rode their horses to death to chase.

I understand, said the Captain. He dabbed at his lips. The coffee was strong enough to stand a spoon in.

So. Anna looked down. She wiped at her eyes with her wrist. She is glad to come back then, from the savages.

They all turned and looked at the little captive. She was singing to herself, slowly, very low, her head nodding a beat at a time, some song in Kiowa. A curse, perhaps, on the enemies of the *Coi-gu*, a plea to the sun which is the father of all things, praise for the Wichita Mountains, a call for help.

She must learn to work again, said Wilhelm. She must learn our ways again. He took a deep breath. We have no children except for a nephew of us who is now working at the cattle establishment of the Englishman in Frio Town. We are prepared to take her in. My wife needs help. There is much work to be done. She doesn't like a chair for sitting? Look at her on the floor.

She thinks she is Indian? asked Anna. She slid her eyes sideways to look at Johanna again. Get up, she said. Johanna ignored her.

I'm afraid so, said the Captain. I hope you will take that into account. She is only ten.

The child must be corrected strong.

I think she's already been through that.

Anna nodded. She is not too small to do her share.

Certainly not, said the Captain.

Wilhelm paused with his mouth slightly open. He was puzzling over something. They waited, as if suspended on strings while his lips worked. Finally he said, And so you have no receipt for the purchasing of that vagon?

No.

THE CAPTAIN SPENT the night lying like a plank on a hard bed upstairs but Johanna would not be moved from the *Curative Waters* wagon bed and her big red *jorongo*. The next day, when all the people came she darted into the barn, swarmed up the ladder with her skirt front tucked into her belt, showing her ankles and shins, and would not come down. When they tried to climb halfway up the ladder and speak to her in German she hurled down a sickle and a barking spud.

Leave her alone, said Captain Kidd. Can you not just leave her alone for a while?

And so the community of D'Hanis celebrated the return of one of their own from the hands of the savages without her. Kind, well-meaning people whose labor had brought about the elegant stone church of St. Dominic's, and graceful stone houses with long gallerias, gardens grown from seeds of the celebrated Huth Seed Company of Castroville, peonies big as cabbages and cabbages the size of butter churns. The priest shook the Captain's hand heartily for several moments, clapped him on the shoulder and expressed his thanks, his admiration, said God surely had protected them that long way. He had an Irish accent. They laid out long tables in the yard, spread with Alsatian foods, smoking briskets in the Texas style, and dishes made of potatoes and cheeses and cream.

Adolph the messenger came to sit beside the Captain. He was a broad-shouldered man with the inevitable squared head of Germany. The dogs had been beaten back under the wagons and lay there with tails thumping steadily in the dust. A bright blue scrub jay darted down to land on the fence palings and look at the food with one eye first and then the other eye, overcome with admiration for the rich look of Alsatian cooking.

The man said, Wilhelm and Anna, they work hard.

The Captain lifted a fluffy biscuit. He said, I'm listening.

They had their nephew staying with them but he ran off. Down to the Nueces strip.

Frio Town.

The same.

Because they worked him like a Turk.

Yes.

The Captain said, What can be done?

Nothing. The man gestured with his big-boned hand toward the crowd with a fork. Everyone has come to celebrate her return. They will go home and talk about it forever, unto the next generation. But they will not come here and ask about her welfare. They will not intrude into the family circle of the Leonbergers and find out if she is in fact being well-treated. Is it not the same with you English?

Unfortunately.

Not anywhere. Not English or Spanish or German. So it is with the world. I am German myself and I tell you, these people can be hard. He let out a long breath. I chased the Indians when they took the girls, killid her parents. I killid my best horse. He blew his lungs out on Bandera Pass.

You did your best. The Captain laid a hand on the man's shoulder and then got up and sat his plate on the tailgate of a wagon. I must go, he said. Thank you for the warning. But I am helpless here.

They have no adoption papers.

Who would care? The priest?

Yes. He would be the one to prepare them I suppose.

Will they adopt her?

The tall man leaned back in his chair and turned his head to look at Wilhelm and Anna. They sat among the crowd of friends and neighbors, stern and cold as if they were at a judicial hearing. The Captain saw that few people were talking to the couple. The guests were laughing and joking among themselves, happy, talkative, and some few were glancing toward the big pole barn where Johanna hid, but they were not talking with the Leonbergers.

The messenger said, No, I do not think they will. Because then they would be legally obligated to support her and according to custom to provide her with a dowry. They did not adopt the nephew.

Well, said the Captain. I understand. He was tightening up inside somehow, his throat seemed to thicken.

The man took hold of the Captain's sleeve. He said, You cannot leave her here.

The Captain felt something close to despair. He said, Thank you sir. Perhaps I could at some time stop for a visit. Now I must be going.

He had to leave, quickly, before tears started running down his face.

TWENTY-ONE

———✦———

H E TURNED BACK the way he had come, drove to the east along the straight-line road, the long twenty-two miles into Castroville. There he stayed at the inn on the Medina and listened all night to the tumbling roar of the grist-mill wheel that turned over the green alluvial water of the Medina River. The next morning he shaved closely and put on his black reading clothes and then went on into San Antonio.

He crossed over Alazan Creek at the ford where he was happy to see Mexican women wading in the water, baskets of wet clothes on their heads, calling and chatting to one another and wringing out their long black hair in the warm April air. They called out saucy things to him in Spanish which they did not think he understood and then cried out in surprise when he answered them back in the same language. They then laughed and splashed water at him and he was very glad to be back in San Antonio.

He was happy also to hear the bells of San Fernando ringing out the hour, and a man whose hair was as white as his own stood up in his buggy and called out, Jefferson Kidd! Come and see me sir! He went down a narrow street of stone houses, hoarding the cool of their courtyards, so that the streets in the center of town were all one long white wall in the style of houses in southern towns since the times of the Romans. Other two-storied houses, *casas de dueña,* town houses for rancheros who had their grazing lands out on the Balcones Heights had second-story balconies of wrought iron that made lacy shadows on the walls below.

It was late evening when he came across the San Martin Street Bridge and then Calamares Street and into the Plaza de Armas. The Spanish Governor's palace, built in 1749 in ruins. There in the wide Plaza de Armas, Military Plaza, were lines of wagons bringing in grain and vegetables and hay to be sold there, and the chili stands with their piles of fruit and simmering cauldrons of chili now lit by lanterns with colored shades. Packed around the square were the commercial establishments, The Vance House, Lessner and Mandelbaum hide dealers, Rhodes and Dean tinware, clothing shops, billiard rooms, carriage repositories. The Captain put the excursion wagon with its promises of curative waters and its bullet holes in a carriage repository and stabled Fancy and Pasha in Haby's stables, each one devouring a great net bag of hay. He checked in at The Vance House and passed a fitful and unhappy night.

The next day he walked out into the Plaza and saw his old print shop next to Advocate Branholme's building. It was now full of broken carriage wheels to be repaired and parts of some kind of machinery. He cupped his hands around his face and looked in; dust on the floor, the Stanhope press sold and gone and probably taken to pieces for parts, a bag of wool scraps, a shoe.

He went next door to Branholme's law office.

Branholme was in, and stood when he saw the Captain. He spoke for thirty minutes or so with the young lawyer about adoption, about the legal status of returned captives, about the Printing Bill.

Branholme said, In a few years perhaps they will rescind the bill. After Davis is gone and after the military is no longer in power. Then it might be feasible to start up your business again. And as for the captives, well, they belong to their parents or guardians.

Captain Kidd then rode Pasha through the traffic, away from the center of town and down the San Antonio River to the ruins of Mission Concepción. Somewhere under layers of legalities they had land there. It was his favorite of all the old missions even though now the main sanctuary was abandoned and scarred with people's names carved into the plaster. He would leave it to Elizabeth. He knew Señor De Lara all too well. The man was a scholar and an expert in Spanish Colonial land grants and his first words would be, But you do not stand to inherit, sir. Only your daughters, and so I will discuss it with them.

He rode back and went to the post office and inquired for letters. He sat down on the steps with the four pages from Elizabeth. He knew her handwriting immediately.

They would come back in two years. *Dearest Papa you know we long for Texas but . . .* She wrote of the long journey and of their weariness, of Olympia's delicacy. They were lacking money and would need to buy horses and who knew how they would now get across the Mississippi? If he had money to send them for the trip, they needed it. Would it be possible to rent the old Betancort house? They were, after all, Mama's people. She had written already to Sr. De Lara concerning the Mission Concepción land.

Newspaper readings would not be well attended here or any big city to the south and east. All the larger cities of Texas had a daily distribution of newspapers fresh from the coast. They came in on the boats at Galveston and Indianola and others came down on the train from St. Louis. Strange to think of children being kidnapped by the Comanche and Kiowa, of attacks by raiding parties, while the telegraph and the steam locomotives marched out of the maw of Progress but so it was. His readings were popular only in small towns in the north and west, like Dallas and Fort McKavett, places near the frontier.

So he bought a new set of newspapers from the Southern cities, the *Memphis Daily Appeal,* the Columbus, Georgia, *Bugle,* along with those from cities in the northeast. He returned to The Vance House and sat up late with his newspapers and smoked and paced the room. He could not sleep. Finally he went down to the lobby and sent a boy out for a pint of whiskey from Milligans. You could trust their whiskey. He loved this town and its river. It was very old. He looked out at the oil-burning streetlamp through the glass of whiskey to see it shiver in tones of gold and brass. *And so am I,* he thought. *But I am not a cripple and I am not stupid.*

THE NEXT MORNING he drove down the Castroville Road with Pasha tied on behind as always. He did not know what to tell himself except that perhaps Anna and Wilhelm just needed the right kind of information or the ability to imagine what it was like for a child taken captive and then redeemed and then adopted by virtual strangers, yes *adopted,* you miserly coldhearted beasts. He would try. Reason, bribery, whatever it took.

Then he would go on north.

It was night by the time he had reached D'Hanis. He turned down the Leonberger farm road and thought that perhaps by this time they would be happy to get rid of her. Maybe not. He had no idea one way or the other. He doubted if they could make her work. Perhaps with severe beatings.

As he came toward the farm he stopped by a grove of mesquite trees. He could see a light shining in the farmhouse window. He sat quietly for a while with his knuckles under his nose, thinking.

Then he saw Johanna alone in the flat, grassy field. She had several heavy leather halters over her shoulder and walked clumsily because of a bucket she held in both hands. They had sent her out into the field alone, after dark, to get the horses. She trudged through the April grass. She was calling to the horses in Kiowa, softly, secretly. She was staggering on the uneven ground, under the weight of the halters and a wooden bucket of shelled corn and her ragged taffy hair flew in strands around her shoulders. She was only ten, sent out into the dark with twenty pounds of halters and corn and the heavy wooden bucket. Into a landscape she did not know.

He stood up. He called to her. Johanna, he said.

She turned. She stopped and stared at the wagon and at

Pasha and himself on the seat. The tall grasses hissed around her skirt hems, the same dress; they had not even offered the girl a bath and a change of clothes.

Kep-dun! A low cry. She turned toward him and paused and then came staggering closer. Oh, Pasha want to eat! Allite? She held out a handful of corn. I giff Pasha, allite? It was the only ploy she could think of to make *Kontah* stop, to make herself welcome, wanted.

He saw dark red stripes across her forearms and hands. It was from the dog whip. The anger that overtook him nearly froze him in place. It almost shut him down. Then he said, calmly, Let's go. It's all right. Let's just go. Drop that goddamn bucket.

He wrapped the reins around the driver's post and stepped down. She dropped the bucket and came running. She grabbed hold of the top rail of the fence and vaulted over it into the road. Her skirts swung up in a flying fan and she landed on her feet.

Kontah, she said. Grandfather. I go with you. She began to cry. I go with you.

Yes, he said. He put his arm around her and then took the halters and hurled them out into the dirt of the road. The Captain turned the *Curative Waters* wagon back toward the north. He said, And if anybody objects we will shoot them full of ten-cent pieces.

TWENTY-TWO

——————————

H E AND JOHANNA drove north again from San Antonio to Wichita Falls and Bowie and Fort Belknap. They traveled sometimes in convoy with the freighters or the Army. He was the man who read the news and she the little captive girl whom he had rescued and who it was said had crept up Indianwise on the depraved animal named Almay as he lay in his hoggish den and before the Captain could restrain her had beaten him to death with a bag of quarters. But look at her now, she has cleaned up quite nicely, uses soap, wears shoes, keeps the Captain's money. They could be seen in wintertime eating houses at a back table as she bent over her book, printing out her letters with a carpenter's pencil on the reverse of one of the Captain's handbills as he patiently guided her hand; A is for Apple, you see my dear, and B is for Boy. When they passed through Dallas the Captain found that Mrs. Gannet had taken up with a man much younger than the Captain, a man only sixty-two, who wore thick glasses and had a waist size of at least forty-four but he lived in Dallas and would stay in Dallas and not go wandering.

Colonel Ranald Mackenzie drove the last holdouts among

the Comanche and the Kiowa to earth in Palo Duro Canyon and thus the Indian Wars came to an end. The Captain and Johanna moved at a reasonable pace through the volatile land of Texas collecting dimes and evading trouble and the Captain read in his clear voice of the new world that had come about while the Americans were fighting their Civil War, of steamships and asteroids and a machine called a typewriter, the new four-in-hand ties. Crime was always popular; shameless sinners, amazing graces. He had the iron tire fixed and sometimes when he was studying over his newspaper articles Johanna would come to stand at his side, take up his watch from where he had laid it on the tailgate, and say, Kep-dun. Time.

Yes, my dear, he said and gathered his marked articles for the reading.

Then they traveled over to the cotton country of Marshall and down to Nacogdoches. And in that town the people came also to hear news from *El Clarion* in Spanish, men in stiff formal black suits and hats in the old Spanish style, rancheros holding on to their lands against all odds, against all Anglos. They lifted their hats to the girl and called her *La Cautiva*.

From there they arrived in East Texas where the former slave population was at last turning to their own lives. Johanna and the Captain drove south along the coast to the Gulf to see the salt sea bringing in its sand-loaded waves and rainbow Portuguese men o' war lying like celluloid cabbages on the beach. At every reading she sat sternly in front of the paint can collecting the money. Gradually she learned the English language and always spoke it with a clipped accent and always had difficulty with the letter *R*. He wrote down words in Kiowa to begin a dictionary of the language but was puzzled as to how to indicate the myriad specific tones and so laid it aside.

The wandering life was amenable to her. Watching the world go by from the safety of the canopy and side curtains, a new town and new people every thirty miles. Bright springs under the shade of the live oaks in the coastal country and sometimes waterless stretches in West Texas from Kerrville to the Llano, and from there to the Concho and Fort McKavett, Wichita Falls and Spanish Fort to see Simon and Doris and their two children.

She never learned to value those things that white people valued. The greatest pride of the Kiowa was to do without, to make use of anything at hand; they were almost vain of their ability to go without water, food, and shelter. Life was not safe and nothing could make it so, neither fashionable dresses nor bank accounts. The baseline of human life was courage. Her gestures and expressions were not those of white people and he knew they never would be. She stared intently when something interested her, her questions were forthright and often embarrassing. All animals were food, not pets. It took a long time before she thought of coins as legal tender instead of ammunition.

In her daily company he found himself also ceasing to value these things that seemed so important to the white world. He found himself falling more deeply into the tales of far places and strange peoples. He asked the news shops to order for him papers from England and Canada and Australia and Rhodesia.

He began to read to his audiences of far places and strange climates. Of the Esquimaux in their seal furs, the explorations of Sir John Franklin, shipwrecks on deserted isles, the long-limbed folk of the Australian Outback who were dark as mahogany and yet had blond hair and made strange music which the writer said was indescribable and which Captain Kidd longed to hear.

He read of the discovery of Victoria Falls and sightings, real or not, of the ghost ship *The Flying Dutchman* and an eyewitness account of a man on the bridge of that ship sending messages by blinking light to them, asking about people long dead. And before these tales for a short time Texans quieted and bent forward to hear. The rain fell, or the snow, or the moon glared down and the lamps failed but they did not notice. At each stop, for an hour or so, Captain Kidd arrested time itself.

The Captain never did understand what had caused such a total change in a little girl from a German household and adopted into a Kiowa one. In a mere four years she completely forgot her birth language and her parents, her people, her religion, her alphabet. She forgot how to use a knife and a fork and how to sing in European scales. And once she was returned to her own people, nothing came back. She remained at heart a Kiowa to the end of her days.

After three years his daughters and his son-in-law and his two grandsons returned to San Antonio, established possession of the now-empty Betancort house, and began the long and nearly hopeless process of trying to recover the Spanish Lands. Emory went in debt for a new press and took over Leon Moke's clothing shop and turned it into a print shop. Olympia sighed and drifted about the rooms of the old Betancort *palacio* until she finally married again, which was a relief to everyone. Elizabeth raised her boys and had a desk in a corner of the long *comedor* overflowing with platte maps and yellowing land records.

When they returned, Captain Kidd finally came in off the roads of Texas. She had made a wanderer of him but all things come to an end. San Antonio had grown and many of the old and beautiful Spanish houses were torn down. The people were despoiled of their lands in ways that broke his heart. Captain Kidd and Johanna came to live with Elizabeth and Emory and their children, his grandsons, he to be old and she to stare into a future unknown. He advised Emory at the print shop where his son-in-law worked with deep interest and delight in his new Babcock cylinder press while the Captain sat at a desk littered with composing sticks and inspected each new print run. Johanna tried to pretend to be a white girl, for his sake. She joined other girls in their excursions on the river, their dancing lessons, and put up with the indignity of riding sidesaddle. She gazed with deep envy at the Mexican women and girls half-naked in Alazan Creek and San Pedro Springs, washing clothes. They slapped water at one another, wrung out their hair, waded with their skirts up around their waists. She sat stiffly in her riding habit and her smart little topper and watched them and rode home and then tried to appear cheerful at dinner, carefully managing her knife and fork and the minute coffee spoon. The Captain sighed heavily, his hands in his lap, staring at his *flan*. The worst had happened. He did not know what to do.

One day John Calley of Durand came riding into the town and stopped to visit with the Captain. His memory of the dignified old gentleman shouting for silence and reason in the mercantile store in Durand had never faded. He stood with his hat shading his face in the hot street named Soledad at the

Betancort double doors. Then the small door set inside the big one came open. A short maid peered out and behind her stood a slender girl of fifteen or so with thick yellow hair braided in a crown. She had blue eyes and a scattering of freckles across her nose. She wore a dress in dark gray with a yellow figure in the weave, a long sweep of hems. Her nails were shell pink and perfectly clean.

Y qué? said the maid in a rude and suspicious voice. *Hágame el favor de decirme lo que quieres, señor.*

Yes? The girl said. Ah you looking for someone?

For a moment he was at a loss for words. Finally: Would you be Johanna, the captive girl the Captain was returning?

Yes, I am Johanna Kidd. She had a small, dubious smile for this stranger in tall traveling boots and a worn duster over his arm.

Calley took off his hat. He couldn't stop looking at her. This had grown out of that grimy ten-year-old staring like a wild animal over the dashboard of the spring wagon, her hair in ragged braids. He remembered how she had slapped the taffy out of his hands.

He said, Ah, yes, well, I stopped by to pay my respects to the Captain. I, ah, happened to be in San Antonio to see about, well, cattle. He paused. Yes, cattle.

Cettinly. She stepped back and lifted one hand to the interior of the old house. She said, He is in the patio just now. Please come in.

He paused with one boot in the air. He said, Do you by any chance remember me?

She regarded him carefully. He stood large and travel-stained and entranced in the cool of the tile-floored hall as she raked him over with a blue stare. I am so sorry, she said, but I am afraid I do not. This way.

His boot heels clicked on the tiles as he followed her and in the sunlight of the patio he saw the Captain reading a thick leather-bound book. After he and the Captain had conversed there in the cool shade of the mimosa, the old man still straight as a wand, he asked if he might call again and so he did. And when he did he brought several newspapers for the Captain and a small, intricate arrangement of dried roses he thought Miss Kidd might like.

Johanna, she said, is very well to call me.

Calley sat down at Elizabeth's small piano and played "Come to the Bower" and "The Yellow Rose of Texas" and did not look up from the keyboard but waited to see if she would come to him and before long she stood at his shoulder. He moved over on the piano bench and after some hesitation she sat down beside him with a graceful arrangement of her skirts and for the first time smiled at him. He taught her the songs, picking them out note by note.

It was for him a long and magical afternoon: the cries of the milkman coming down the street with his quiet gray horse shouting *Leche! Leche bronca!* and somebody calling for Timotea at the big wooden Veramendi doors and the Devil's trumpet vine with its blatant red cornets drooping over the closed shutters and making shadowy gestures as the wind came up off the river behind the house. Calley sang in his off-key raspy voice, *She walks along the river in the quiet summer night . . .* and then forgot the lyrics but was fairly sure it had something to do with stars, bright. After a while he stopped and just sat and looked at her.

The Captain stood at one of the tall windows, a window that started at the floor and went up to nine feet, and watched the milkman and his horse walk past one of the old Spanish houses that were being demolished, past the new brick buildings around the Plaza de las Islas, into the hot afternoon, into history.

When Calley finally had to leave at sunset she stood at the door with his hat between her two hands like a great felted cake.

She said, carefully, Heah is you hat. We would be very heppy if you would come to dinnah.

John Calley decided to remain in South Texas and gather wild cattle out of the area around Frio Town, south of San Antonio in the brush country, in the notorious Nueces Strip. The reason few people did that was that it was an area devoid of law and not for the faint of heart, but if a man could stay alert and live long enough he could gather enough wild cattle to make a small fortune. It depended on how well you could shoot and how deeply you did or did not sleep. He hired men like Ben Kinchlowe who was hard as nails and spoke both English and Spanish and was accomplished in the handling of both cattle and revolvers. He branded all he gathered with a road brand and went north and after two trips John Calley was a made man.

He and Johanna were married in the Betancort house according to the old Southern custom of being married in the bride's home and in January. Johanna and the Captain sat up in her bedroom, on the bed, waiting to be called downstairs. There Calley waited in a stiff black cutaway and striped ascot with the Episcopal minister from St. Joseph's. Her hands were shaking.

She sat close beside him as if for protection against an

unknown future; she smelled of the whitebrush blossoms that grew along Calamares Creek and orange water and the starch of her gown.

Kontah, she said. Her voice quavered. Tears stood in her eyes unshed.

It's all right, Johanna.

I have nevah been marriet before.

No! Really?

Pliss, Kep-dun. She pressed with a trembling hand at her elaborate braiding and the veil pulled over a rim of beaded wire. Don't make chokes. I am faint. John has never been marriet before eithah. Her round face was red and the freckles stood out like spotting on a hill country peach.

By God let us hope not.

Kontah, what is the best rules for being marriet?

Well, he said. One, don't scalp anybody. Two, do not eat with your hands. Do not kill your neighbor's chickens. He tried to keep his tone light. His throat was closing up and he made harsh noises as he cleared it. As for the positive commandments, you two will figure them out for yourselves. It will be all right, it will be all right.

He slipped the old gold hunting watch out of his pocket and clicked it open and held it out to her.

She wiped at her eyes and looked down at it and said, It is eleven. Time, *Kontah.*

Elizabeth called up the stairs and then ran up, holding her skirts. She put in her head and she was smiling. Johanna, she said. Are you ready?

Johanna turned and put her arms around the Captain's neck. We will come to visit often, she said. You are my cuuative watah. Then she began to sob.

Yes, he said. He shut his eyes and prayed he would not start crying himself. And you are my dearest little warrior. You must not cry. He pressed the watch into her hand. I would like for you to have it. Time seems to have been sweeping ahead very fast these last years. How many years I worried about you and also delighted in your company. And now it is time for me to give you away.

AFTER SHE AND John Calley were married she went with him on the next drive, all the way to Sedalia, Missouri, driving a light four-wheel buggy. It was a life she could love. And so Johanna and John Calley rode the cattle country of Texas together into the next century. And lived to see an airplane land in Uvalde. They held hands alongside their two grown children to see it strike the Texas earth and the pilot walk away from the wreckage as if he had done it on purpose.

The Captain drifted into a very old age and worked again at the Kiowa dictionary until he found it hard to see. Often he remembered her cry at the Great Brazos River Ten-Cent Shootout. It had been a war cry, and she had been only ten, and she had meant it.

Britt Johnson and Paint Crawford and Dennis Cureton were killed by the Comanche in 1871, on a freighting trip near Graham in North Texas. They were caught on the only open stretch between Graham and Indian Mound Mountain. They were buried where they fell and there their gravestone stands to this day.

Simon and Doris raised a family of six children, all of whose names started with the letter *D*. They were all musicians and the family traveled around North Texas bringing Irish jigs and cowboy ballads to barn dances and fairs for many years. The Horrells continued their crime spree in central Texas and New Mexico until several of them were killed in the great Lampasas Square Shoot-Out in 1877 and they finally made the Eastern papers.

San Fernando cathedral received a new front with twin towers but the old sanctuary and dome over the altar, built in 1733, remained unchanged. The *camposanto* graves had to be moved south of the San Antonio River but many of the original Spanish settlers had been buried under the floor and so there lie the bones of the Betancorts, perhaps content at last in this New World with the bells of San Fernando ringing out the aves and the angeluses. The bones of the Kiowa warriors did not lie in the earth but in the stories of their lives, told and retold—their bravery and daring, the death of Britt Johnson and his men, and Cicada, the little girl taken from them by the Indian Agent, Three Spotted's little blue-eyed girl.

In his will the Captain asked to be buried with his runner's badge. He had kept it since 1814. He said he had a message to deliver, contents unknown.

A NOTE FROM THE AUTHOR

Anyone interested in the psychology of children captured and adopted by Native American tribes on the frontier should read Scott Zesch's book *The Captured*. It is excellent. His book documents child captives from the Texas frontier, including his own great-great-uncle, and in each instance gives the background of death and terror these children endured before they were adopted or claimed within the tribe. There has not been a definitive study of the psychological strategies these children adopted in order to survive but one would be welcome. They apparently became Indian in every way and rarely readjusted when returned to their non-native families. They always wished to return to their adoptive families, even when they had been with their Indian families for less than a year. This was true for both the Anglo, German-Anglo, and Mexican children taken. I think the words of my Irish character Doris Dillon best expressed it. I'll let you find her words in the story.

ACKNOWLEDGMENTS

As always much gratitude to my agent, Liz Darhansoff, and editor, Jennifer Brehl, who gave their immediate and unstinting support to this story.

Thanks to June and Wayne Chism for the story of Wayne's ancestor Caesar Adolphus Kydd, who was the original reader of the news in small towns in North Texas in the 1870s and was the inspiration for the Captain both in *The Color of Lightning* and in this book.

About the author

About the book

Insights,
Interviews
& More...

Read on

Meet Paulette Jiles

Jill Gann Photography

PAULETTE JILES is a poet, memoirist, and bestselling novelist. Her books include *Cousins*, a memoir, and the novels *Enemy Women*, *Stormy Weather*, *The Color of Lightning*, and *Lighthouse Island*. She lives on a ranch near San Antonio, Texas. ∿

Reading Group Discussion Questions

1. Discuss Captain Jefferson Kyle Kidd's work as a newspaper reader. What does he bring to his audience, and what does he gain from his work besides financial compensation?

2. Why does Kidd accept the difficult job of returning Johanna home? What drives him to complete the job despite the danger and obstacles?

3. Why do you think Johanna wants to stay with her Kiowa family? What do you think she remembers of her life before she was taken?

4. What connects Kidd to Johanna? Why does she seem to trust him so easily?

5. What does Kidd worry may become of Johanna once she's returned to her family? What does he know of the fate of other "returned captives"?

6. Doris Dillion says that Johanna is "carried away on the flood of the world," and is "not real and not not-real." She describes her as having "been through two creations" and "forever falling." Do you agree with her assessment? Does Johanna remain this way through the course of the novel? ▶

Reading Group Discussion Questions
(continued)

7. Discuss the various tensions in the novel: Indians and whites, soldiers and civilizations, and America's recent past and its unsure future. In what ways do these tensions underlie the story of Kidd and Johanna?

8. Imagine the perspective of Johanna's Kiowa family. Why, do you think, they would've taken her in and raised her? Why would they give her up? How do you think they felt when they let her go?

9. Partway through his journey with Johanna, Kidd feels as though he was "drawn back into the stream of being because there was once again a life in his hands." What do you think this means? What does it tell you about Kidd's emotional life? ∾

Essay on Research

LIKE MANY WRITERS, I can get lost in the joys of research. Just using Bing to search images of "photographs; Comanche and Kiowa captives" brought up a lot of great photos from the Smithsonian photo archives, and the temptation is to go to the Smithsonian photo files and wander about there for an entire morning. It was there that I found a photo of Kiowa Dutch—a mysterious person who was clearly Caucasian but had been raised Kiowa, and had no knowledge of his original name or birthplace or provenance.

For Simon the fiddler I asked a lot of questions of the fiddler in my little bluegrass group, Tom Bomer. In fact Simon is more or less based on Tom, who is really a first-rate country fiddler, and I have not yet told him the alarming news that he is in one of my books.

As for the landscape of North Texas, I had already explored the remains of Spanish Fort for *The Color of Lightning*. It is on the Red River. There is nothing like being there, walking among the old foundations and visiting the graveyard on a rise just outside Spanish Fort, overlooking the Red. It is beautiful country and the water of the river is really very red.

For the old Spanish/Canary Islander families of San Antonio, I have been familiar with their history for a long time. My husband's first wife—and therefore my step-grandchildren—was directly ▶

Essay on Research *(continued)*

descended from the first mayor of San Antonio, Juan Leal Goraz (1731). I researched their genealogy because I wanted the grandchildren to know what an interesting and wonderful family history they had. I never thought I would use this in one of my books, but it simply came to hand when I needed it, as does much random research.

The Catholic Church records described peoples' coloring, and many Canary Islanders had gray eyes (*ojos claros*). The missions and the old structures of San Antonio have been my delight for many years, and Concepción (Mission Nuestra Señora de la Purísima Concepción) is, I think, the finest of the three mission churches—although it is not as well-known as San Jose.

As for the Spanish land grant, again, this was in my husband's first wife's family—Maria Luisa Leal (great-granddaughter of Juan Leal Goraz) was granted land in the Navarro tract, south of San Antonio, but I was never able to trace what happened to it. The small towns of Castroville and D'Hanis are on Highway 90, the old road that went from San Antonio to El Paso. This is now of course a modern highway, and I drive through both every time I go into San Antonio to go to the airport.

Researching is great fun—sometimes it is armchair exploration and takes you to far places while you are safe at home in the air-conditioning. Other times just have to be there—there is no substitute for walking in the landscape itself, or turning over dusty old pages in the archives of San Antonio. ⌒

Excerpt from
The Color of Lightning

Chapter 1

WHEN THEY FIRST CAME into the country it was wet and raining and if they had known of the droughts that lasted for seven years at a time they might never have stayed. They did not know what lay to the west. It seemed nobody did. Sky and grass and red earth as far as they could see. There were belts of trees in the river bottoms and the remains of old gardens where something had once been planted and harvested and then the fields abandoned. There was a stone circle at the crest of a low ridge.

Moses Johnson was a stubborn and secretive man who found statements in the minor prophets that spoke to him of the troubles of the present day. He came to decisions that could not be altered. He read aloud: *Therefore thus saith the Lord: Ye have not harkened unto me in proclaiming liberty, every one to his own brother, and every man to his neighbor. Behold, I proclaim a liberty for you, saith the Lord, to the sword, to the pestilence, and to the famine, and I will make you to be removed into all the kingdoms of the earth.* That's in Jeremiah, he said. So they ▶

7

Excerpt from *The Color of Lightning* (continued)

left Burkett's Station, Kentucky, in 1863 in four wagons, fifteen white people and five black including children, to get away from the war between armies and also the undeclared war between neighbors.

Britt Johnson was proud of his wife and he loved her and was deeply jealous of her because of her good looks and her singing voice and her unstinting talk and laughter. Her singing voice. All along their journey from Kentucky to north Texas he had been afraid for her. Afraid that some white man, or black, or Spaniard, would take a liking to her and he would have to kill him. He rode a gray saddle horse always within sight of the wagon that carried her and the children. She was as much of grace and beauty as he would ever get out of Kentucky.

Before they crossed the Mississippi at Little Egypt they stopped and there at the heel of the free state of Illinois Moses Johnson caused Britt's manumission papers to be drawn up and notarized by a shabby consumptive justice of the peace who looked as if these papers were the last ones he would notarize before he died from sucking in the damp malarial air and the smoke of a black cigar.

The justice of the peace said it was a shame to manumit the man, look at what a likely buck he was, a great big strong nigger, and Moses Johnson said, You are going to meet your Maker before long, sir. You will meet him with tobacco on your breath and smelling of the Indian devil weed, and what will you say to Him who is the Author of your being? You will say Yes I did my utmost to keep a human being in the bonds of slavery and robbed of his liberty, and moreover I spent my precious breath a-smoking of filthy black cigars. Here is the lawyer's signature on his papers and his wife's papers as well. You will have your clerk copy all of these and then deposit the copies in the Pulaski County Courthouse. And from there they went on to Texas.

You could raise cattle anywhere in that country. At that time there was very little mesquite or underbrush, just the bluestem and the grama grasses and the low curling buffalo grass and the wild oats and buckwheat. When the wind ran over it they all bent in various yielding flows, with the wild buckwheat standing in islands, stiff with its heads of grain and red branching stems. The lower creek bottoms were like parks, with immense trees and no underbrush. The streams ran clearer than they do now. The grass held the soil in tight fists of roots. The streams did not always run but here and there were water holes whose edges were cut up with hoof marks of javelina and buffalo and sometimes antelope. Ducks flashed up off the surface and skimmed away in their flight patterns of beating and sailing, beating and sailing.

Mary had been raised in the main house with old Mrs. Randall who was blind in one eye, and she had not wanted to come to Texas, even on the promise of her freedom. Britt said he would make it up to her. As soon as the country was settled and the war was over he would start in as a freighter. He would break in a team from some of the wild mustangs that ran loose in the plains. There had to be a way to catch them. Then he would buy heavy horses. And then they would have a good house and a big fenced garden and a cookstove and a kerosene lamp.

The people who had come from Burkett's Station built their houses with large stone fireplaces and chimneys. They rode out into the country to explore. The tall grass hissed around the horses' legs like spray. Feral cattle ran in spotted and elusive herds, their horns as long as lances, splashed in red and white and some of them dotted like clown cattle.

They had come to live on the very edge of the great Rolling Plains, with the forested country behind them and the empty lands in front. Long, attentive lines of timber ran like lost regiments along the rivers and creeks. Everything was strange to them: the cactus in all its hooked varieties, the elusive antelope in white bibs and black antlers, the red sandstone dug up in plates to build chimneys and fireplaces big enough to get into in case there was a shooting situation.

There were nearly fifty black people in Young County now. Britt said soon they could have their own church and their own school. Mary was silent for a moment as the thought struck her and then cried out, She could be the Elm Creek teacher! She could teach children to sing their ABCs and recite Bible verses! For instance how the people ▶

9

Excerpt from *The Color of Lightning* *(continued)*

were freed from Babylon in Isaiah! Britt nodded and listened as he stood in the doorway.

Mary planned the school and the lessons aloud and at length, and lit the fire and sang and talked and made up rhymes for the children that had been born to them, Jim the oldest and Jube who was nine and Cherry, age five, who had wavy hair like her mother. She told the children stories of who they were. That their great-grandfather had been brought from Africa, from a place called Benin, and that he was the son of a great king there, taken captive when he was ten, because he saw in the distance a waving red silk flag and had gone to see who was waving it in such an inviting way. He had sung a certain song he wanted all his descendants to remember but it had been forgotten. From time to time Mary said she dreamed about Kentucky and the rain there, and her mother and her aunts. She dreamed that she and Britt and the children had gone home.

BRITT TRIED NOT to favor Jim over the other two but already at age eleven the boy was both manly and kind. Jim bent over the pages of the Bible by firelight, entranced by words like *reigneth* and *strowed*. His mother made him spell them out. That spring Jim rode with his father searching out the wild cattle that grazed along the Clear Fork of the Brazos and when they came upon buffalo they sat on their horses and watched them, looking for some clue as to their nature. One of the white men who had lived in the country for ten years led them to see a herd moving north in the cold spring rain. They were dark and woolly and stood high at the shoulder, they moved down the slopes of the Brazos Valley wreathed in their own steam and water dripping from their half-moon horns, free and untended. No human beings owned them or directed their movement. They went where they meant to go in their own minds. They spread to the bald horizon under a drifting animal mist, and they smelled good.

"I wonder if they have regular teeth," said Moses.

"Like cows," said old man Peveler. "They just have regular teeth like cows."

"How do they eat?"

"They eat very well. The tongue especially."

Young Jim wanted to ride down among them but Britt laid his hand on the boy's forearm and shook his head. A calf turned to stare at them. It was a bright rusty red. Its mother turned and called to it and the calls from the herd of thousands in low explosive grunts made a ceaseless web of sound as the herd made their way north by the notions they held unspoken and secret, some ageless living map written out invisibly in their hearts.

They turned back toward Elm Creek. Old man Peveler had been in the country a long time and carried the scar of an arrow wound in his neck. The red men live in the north, he told them. Past the West Fork of the Trinity and on beyond the Red River, which is four days' ride north of here. That is their land and this is their raiding country. They raid for fun. The young men love it. Then they ride back north across the Red and they are safe there, so keep your firearms loaded and to hand.

And so they stayed. In Kentucky there was nothing but war and no safe place. To the north and west were the wild Indian lands of plain and canyon. Now that they had arrived they found that there was no other place to go. There was no retreat. No going back.

Britt worked for old man Peveler, driving freight, carrying supplies from Weatherford over the rolling prairies to Fort Belknap and Concho, supplies to the Ledbetter Salt Works. This way he learned the roads and the freighting business. The men at these places told him that he should be careful. But Moses Johnson said he hadn't seen a red man since they had arrived. Judge Wilson said it was true, there had been some kind of Indians close by at some time but he did not know of what persuasion they were and they were gone now, and with nearly two hundred civilized people in the county it was not likely they would return.

They were alone now. All those who had come from Burkett's Station, Kentucky, were alone, each family in its own house on the ocean of grass. Their cabin windows sparked in the night like the ▶

Excerpt from *The Color of Lightning* (continued)

distant ports of small craft on unfamiliar seas. They were not sure what lay to the north and west, perhaps some veiled landscape or nation of people who had once owned the land where they themselves now lived. But these people were gone and were not coming back.

BRITT LAY DOWN his tin shears and listened. It was a heavy dark night with a haze about the three-quarter moon, hot and close. The dog stood up and stalked slowly into the yard with the fur of his back rising hair by hair. Mary and the children were asleep. The trumpet vine crawled down over the doorway and in it some persistent ticking insect clocked the seconds. Britt stepped to one side of the open door, into the shadow where he could not be seen, with a half-made candle sconce in his hands. A wind came up out of the grasslands and moved down into the valley of Elm Creek and rattled the cottonwood leaves over the cabin. The dog stood stiff-legged, staring at the far bluff of the creek where the stone circle was. A man stood there. In the blue moonlight Britt could see that the top half of his face was painted black. His hair drifted in the wind. Then he was gone.

THE MORNING OF October 13, 1864, Britt bridled his team of horses. The men were going to Weatherford for supplies and a few other things like hard candy and Mrs. Fitzgerald's hair dye. There are no mornings anywhere like mornings in Texas, before the heat of the day, the world suspended as if it were early morning in paradise and fading stars like night watchmen walking the periphery of darkness and calling out that all is well. Mary's lessons scraped clean from the thin boards, and bread baking in a skillet.

Britt came in and took up a smoking hot triangle of cornbread from the skillet and lifted it to his mouth. Then he bent forward with a confused expression to a piece of paper lying on the clothes trunk. All over the margins of the paper were sums.

Their freedom papers.

She had been using the margins of their freedom papers to teach the children to write sums with a pen.

Britt slung the cornbread back into the skillet and shouted her name. How did she ever think she could do such a thing? What white man would now believe these papers were real? Mary shouted to him he could go and get another set. How were the children supposed to learn how to use a pen? There wasn't any other paper. She stalked across the cabin with her chin in the air and her hair coming unpinned from under her headcloth. She banged the skillet onto the hearth and pieces of cornbread flew up and scattered.

Britt stormed outside and threw his dray whip across the yard. He turned and went back in again. How could he go and ask Moses Johnson for another set? And let him know how he did not value them, but let the children scribble and blot ink all over them? Moses Johnson nearly got himself lynched for wanting to free his slaves, his life's mortal end could have been in those papers. Look at them. Just look. He held up the manumission papers. Seven times nine equals sixty-three, seven times seven equals forty-nine. Divide by three. A hot feeling rose into his chest and then to his face.

"You were looking for a better life than I could give you," he shouted. "You'd rather be a house slave to old Mrs. Randall than to be free in Texas with me."

If she didn't like the way he lived his life she could go back to Kentucky to her mother and take the children with her, war or no war. The children hid in the washhouse and spied with fixed stares out the cracks between the logs and whispered to each other about the progress of the fight between their parents.

Britt lowered his head and bit his upper lip to keep from saying anything more, and when he raised it again Mary had run over to the window and thrown open the shutters. Her arms were crossed and she was staring out at the grapevines draping over the heavy green water of Elm Creek.

"And stop looking at yourself in the mirror," he said. "And when you go, leave Jim with me."

Mary took the mirror from the wall and threw it on the floor. It broke up into many angled pieces. Each piece reflected something of their ▶

house and the clothing of their children hung on pegs on the wall, and one large piece shone with the image of the sky and its early-morning adornment of cottony clouds overhead tumbling southeast in the early breeze and the bright dots of cottonwood leaves.

Two married people found themselves on separate and barren planets, alone in a place called Young County in the remote land of Texas. In an instant they realized that the bonds between them were not strong at all, but very fragile, and if these were broken they would be solitary and isolated for all eternity, and all that they had made together and the children they had made between them would be thrown out on long orbits like minor comets.

"I don't want the damn thing and I never wanted it the minute you brought it home. Don't ask me if I'm sorry because I ain't sorry and I never will be sorry." She kicked at the broken pieces. "There ain't nothing wrong with those papers because I could scrape it all off if I wanted to, Britt Johnson, and besides they are going to end the war and free everybody and those papers won't mean nothing, nothing, listen to me. You never listen, Britt. You are half deaf, I don't know which half, maybe it switches from one ear to the other depending which side I am standing on. And I wouldn't mind going home at all, no sir I would not. Next wagon going east I would, I can cook and earn my way as well as anybody."

"Woman, will you never shut up?"

They were both caught up in a rage of destruction, both hoping that at some point the other would realize how serious this was.

Britt turned and left. He walked straight out to the corral and pulled the lead rope from its pullaway knot and got on Cajun's back. He caught up Duke's lead rope in his right hand. He bent his head for a moment and thought about the other black people he would see in Weatherford. He named them to himself as if the names were a kind of secret, personal magic against the desolation he saw in front of him which was his life, if she indeed were to leave, without her, and without Cherry and Jube. At the last moment young Jim bolted out of the washhouse and in one clean leap sat himself on Duke's back.

Mary stood in the doorway. She was crying.

"And don't bring me back nothing," she said.

He turned the leader out onto the road. "All right," he said.

"I don't want to go back to Kentucky," she said.

"All right."

AT THE FITZGERALD home Britt slid off his saddle horse Cajun and lifted his hat to the people gathered there. Young Jim lifted his hat as well but remained on Duke's back.

"Mrs. Fitzgerald, Mrs. Durgan," Britt said. "Good morning, Mr. Johnson, Mr. Peveler, Judge."

"Good morning, Britt," they said.

"Well, Britt, I hate to see you hitch up that good saddle horse," said old man Peveler.

"I'll have me a team," said Britt. "Before too long." He lifted the harness onto Cajun's back.

Mrs. Fitzgerald was a large woman who had been married in East Texas to a man named Carter who was half black and then she was widowed in some dubious way, and had come out to the Red River country with her son and daughter and son-in-law and two granddaughters. After Carter died then she married a man named Fitzgerald and then he died of tertiary fever. Her ranch house was two stories, built of horizontal logs and plastered over an eggshell white. It had a wide veranda all around and immense cottonwoods sighing overhead now illuminated by fall leaves the color of lemons. She had a view toward the architectural arrangements of red stone in the bluffs of the Brazos and Indian Mound Mountain. Her son-in-law had been shot dead in some kind of argument over property lines. Elizabeth Fitzgerald now ran the place single-handed with her powerful, carrying voice and bottomless energy. Her daughter, Susan Durgan, and the two granddaughters stayed close to the ranchhouse while Mrs. Fitzgerald rode out sidesaddle to harass her hired hands all day. Her twelve-year-old son Joe Carter rode out with her but stayed twenty yards behind. At present Elizabeth was boxed into a stiff, loud dress, ▶

and her vast waistline was armored with a whalebone corset.

"Don't you give Mr. Graham any more than five cents a pound for that dirty salt of his!" she shouted.

"Yes ma'am," said Moses Johnson. His voice was low and resigned. He cleared his throat.

Two of Fitzgerald's heavy wheelers stood in the corral unharnessed and calling out to the other horses. The Fitzgerald team were solid bays and when they sweated the sweat came out in rosettes on their necks like leopard spots. They were her best horses and she would not permit them to be used for a short trip to Weatherford and so instead they backed a pair of half-broke chestnuts into the traces and then placed Britt's light leaders in front of the two-ton freight wagon.

Jim jumped down and stood aside as his father's horses were backed into place. The men got aboard. They would cross Elm Creek and the water would swell the wood of the freight wagons, the felloes and the axles. They would journey on for a day to Weatherford with tight wheel spokes and undercarriages.

"Didn't Mary send you with no dinner?" Elizabeth Fitzgerald stormed up to Britt where he sat on the wagon seat and peered at the space at his feet. Her big yellow-and-pink-checkered skirts flew out around her feet.

"No ma'am," he said.

"Well, Britt." Elizabeth nodded. "Y'all been fighting. I won't have it, I won't have it."

"Mrs. Fitzgerald." He lifted a hand. "I can fight with my own wife if I want."

"Leave young Jim with me," she said. "I'll get something for you." She turned back to the house. When she came out with a parcel of food wrapped in a tea towel she said, "Leave young Jim here. I'll send him over to bring Mary and the little ones to stay with me while you're gone."

"Yes ma'am," said Britt. "Jim, you hear?" He watched as his son Jim, in bitter disappointment, wrung his hat between his hands and stalked off to the house.

"Joe ain't going either so no sulking!" Elizabeth shouted after him.

Joe Carter and Jim slunk away toward the creek in a loose adolescent walk and kicked at stones and horse manure.

Moses Johnson glanced at Britt and then to Judge Wilson.

"I guess she don't care for you going all the way to Weatherford." Moses' raspy low voice was thick with the heavy pollen in the air. His lips worked with the effort of not saying anything more.

"It ain't that," said Britt.

"Well." Moses shifted the reins from hand to hand. The two lead horses shifted the straight-bar driving bits in their mouths. They were impatient to go. The cool wind was inviting. ▶

Excerpt from *The Color of Lightning* (continued)

"You could bring her back something fine from Weatherford," he said.

Britt looked ahead at the road. "Maybe that would help. I don't know."

And so they started and the water of the creek flashed up in sprays around them, flew out in arcs from the passage of the wheels, the pools dotted with cottonwood leaves. Overhead the sandhill cranes and the great white egrets drifted like ash in shifting planes, heading south. ∽

Discover great authors, exclusive offers, and more at hc.com.